Outstanding Praise for *Lily's Crossing*
A Newbery Honor Book
A *Boston Globe–Horn Book* Honor Book
An ALA Notable Children's Book

"With Ms. Giff's usual easygoing language and swift, short paragraphs, the impact of the war on an American child is brilliantly told."　　　　—*The New York Times Book Review*

★ "Details . . . are woven with great effect into a realistic story."　　　　—*The Horn Book Magazine*, Starred

"Fully satisfying. . . . This is a fine piece of historical fiction that evokes a time and place without sacrificing or taking advantage of its characters' emotional lives."
　　　　　　　　　—*The Bulletin*, Recommended

"With wry comedy and intense feeling . . . Giff gets across a strong sense of what it was like on the home front during World War II. . . . The friendship story is beautifully drawn."
　　　　　　　　　—*Booklist*

"Giff's well-drawn, believable characters and vivid prose style make this an excellent choice." —*School Library Journal*

"[A] deftly told story."　　　　　　　—*Kirkus Reviews*

"Exceptional characterizations and a robust story line. . . . Closely observed, quickly paced and warmly told, this has all the ingredients that best reward readers."
　　　　　　　　　—*Publishers Weekly*

Patricia Reilly Giff is the author of many beloved books for children, including the Kids of the Polk Street School books, the Friends and Amigos books, and the Polka Dot Private Eye books. Her novels for middle-grade readers include *The Gift of the Pirate Queen* and the Casey, Tracy & Company books. She lives in Weston, Connecticut.

Lily's Crossing

PATRICIA REILLY GIFF

A YEARLING BOOK

Published by
Dell Yearling
an imprint of
Random House Children's Books
a division of
Random House, Inc.
1540 Broadway
New York, New York 10036

Visit us on the Web! www.randomhouse.com/kids

Educators and librarians, for a variety of teaching tools, visit us at
www.randomhouse.com/teachers

ISBN: 0-440-41453-9

Reprinted by arrangement with Delacorte Press

Printed in the United States of America

February 1999

20   19   18   17   16   15   14   13   12

OPM

For Jim,
and for the people I loved
in St. Albans and
Rockaway . . .

THE AUTHOR WISHES TO THANK
THE MACDOWELL COLONY.

Lily's Crossing

Chapter 1

St. Albans, 1944

*L*ily Mollahan's bedroom was at the top of the stairs, the only one on the second floor. "The top of the house," Gram always told her, "the top of the world."

Lily sank back on her heels to look around at the blue walls and ceiling, and the gold stars pasted on here and there. Then she stretched up again, working with Poppy's paint scraper, to peel off a star that was almost beyond her reach.

She was hot and sticky, the temperature at least ninety

degrees, and Gram, who didn't have one bit of patience, was calling from the kitchen for the tenth time.

"Your father will be home in just a few minutes, and the table isn't set."

As if Lily didn't know it was dinnertime. Even Mrs. Curley halfway down 200th Street would be able to smell that cabbage cooking. "I thought you wanted me to finish packing," Lily called back as loudly as she could, to drown out the radio in the kitchen.

She could hardly breathe in that bedroom, Lily thought, glancing around again; she could hardly walk. Things were pulled out all over the floor, waiting to be stuffed into her suitcase: books, papers with stories she had written, bathing suits, and heaps of clothes Gram had put on the bed.

She had even found an old silver mirror of her mother's she had hidden away in back of the closet last winter. She was going to put it carefully on top of the suitcase in a nest of pajamas. It would be a miracle if she ever got that far, though, if everything got itself sorted out, and packed, and if they made it to the house in Rockaway before her birthday on Monday.

"Rockaway." She said it aloud, loving the sound of it on her tongue. Rockaway and the ocean were waiting for her. The summer without homework . . . to write stories for herself and not Sister Eileen. The summer without a piano to practice every afternoon. Days and days to sneak into the movies with her best friend, Margaret.

2

Gram was at the bottom of the stairs now, the six o'clock news blaring from the radio behind her. War news, about D-Day. The invasion of France by the Allies a couple of weeks ago. That was all anybody talked about. No, not quite. Sister Eileen was much more interested in whether the class had rosaries and clean handkerchiefs in their pockets than in who was going to win the war.

Too bad about Sister Eileen. Lily would be out of St. Albans in four days, and Sister Eileen would still be stuck there in St. Pascal's thinking about everyone's clean handkerchiefs.

"Lily? You're not packed yet?" Gram called. "I thought you'd finished an hour ago. And remember we don't have that much room in the car."

"Almost finished," Lily said, and "almost started," under her breath. And there, with another slide of the paint scraper, the star came off the wall in one piece, drifting into her outstretched palm. It was perfect, the points still as sharp as when they were new. The star she had scraped off last year had torn a little, and . . .

Lily turned it over. A trace of glue was still on the back. She put her mouth against it, a kiss. Her mother had been the last one to touch that spot when she had pasted it up for her years ago. She had still been Baby Elizabeth then . . . no one had called her Lily yet, and her mother had been alive . . . "playing the piano with you on her lap," Poppy had told her once, "dancing in the

3

living room with you on her shoulder." Lily wished she could remember it.

She could hear her father coming now, whistling along 200th Street, just off the Q3A bus, calling hello to Mrs. Bruns. Gram heard him too. "Dinner this minute, Lily," she said, clumping back toward the kitchen.

Lily stood up and put the star in between two pages of her book, *Evangeline*. By this time, Poppy was in the kitchen; she could hear him talking to Gram. Lily raced down for a hug before Gram started to talk and talk, and no one else could get a word in edgewise.

Poppy was standing at the sink, his straw hat still on but pushed back, drinking a glass of water from the tin measuring cup. Lily loved to drink out of that too. It always made the water taste icy, even on the hottest day.

Her father turned. "Lily Billy," he said, smiling at her. "All packed? Ready for Rockaway?"

"Ready," she said.

Gram rolled her eyes in back of Poppy, but Lily didn't even blink. She slid some plates around the table, the forks and the knives, while Poppy tossed his hat over the hook on the door and washed his hands.

"I have a surprise," he said over his shoulder. "You won't believe—"

"Mr. Egan is a Nazi spy," Lily said at the same minute.

Poppy stopped to listen to what she was saying. He always did that. It was one of his nicest ways. He was biting his lip, though, almost as if he'd laugh.

4

Gram speared the boiled beef out of the pot and dripped it across the counter to the cutting board. "Mr. Egan is not a spy," she said. "I've told you that about fourteen times. Mr. Egan is—"

"A spy," Lily said, her eyes narrowed at Gram.

"Well," said Poppy, "I'll have to keep my eye on him while you and Gram are in Rockaway."

"You'll be with us on some weekends," Lily said. "He could—"

"And what do you think poor Tom Egan is doing?" Gram asked, slicing into the meat.

"He's building something in his garage," Lily said.

"Certainly sounds suspicious," said Poppy, grinning.

"It could be anything," Lily said. "When he saw me looking in the window, he said I was into everyone's business."

"True," said Gram.

"You have to be alert," Poppy said.

Lily slid into her seat, smiling. She knew he was teasing. "You said you had a surprise," she reminded him.

"The piano," said Poppy.

Lily took a deep breath. "I'll miss it this summer." She crossed her fingers.

Gram turned to look at her quickly over her shoulder.

"I love music." Lily stared right back. Music, yes, she thought, but not the piano. The damn piano, she called it deep inside her head. If Gram ever thought she even knew that word, she'd be in trouble for a month.

"Like your mother." Poppy pulled a chair out across from her. "Well, you won't have to be without the piano this summer."

Lily looked down at the damp beef Gram was putting on her plate, the pale cabbage, the boiled potatoes with a sprig of parsley from the Victory garden in back. "But how . . ."

Poppy was nodding. "Not only the piano, but an extra suitcase full of stuff if you like. I've hired a truck—"

"A truck?" Gram said. "What will that cost?"

Poppy waved his hand around. "Lily has a birthday coming up," he said. "I just couldn't resist."

Lily looked down at her plate, three piles of stuff, cabbage, and beef, and potatoes. She knew Poppy was waiting for her to say something. He was waiting for her to throw her arms around him and tell him how wonderful it was. She could hardly talk, though. She picked up her knife and cut her beef into a bunch of little pieces. "Amazing," she said at last.

"Yes, it is," said Gram.

Chapter 2

It was Friday afternoon. School was over. Goodbye, St. Pascal's, goodbye, Sister Eileen, goodbye, report card. Lily had put the report card in Gram's hand at the front door, walked right past her and up to her bedroom. Forty things were left to jam into a cardboard box.

Lily put the first one in, a bottle of lily-of-the-valley perfume, used up except for a little darkish stuff at the bottom. It smelled delicious, though. She waited to put the next thing in; she could hear Gram's footsteps on the stairs. She kept her back stiff, staring down at the bottle. She knew what was coming. "D in music," Gram would say. "How could you possibly . . ." And she would have spotted that effort mark, B−, too. In fact, she'd say the whole thing was a disgrace.

Lily took a breath. Someone was knocking at the front door, banging on the door. She could hear Gram's footsteps stop, could picture her turning . . .

Lily rushed to the window. Downstairs was the truck, gray, rusty: MCHUGH'S—WE'LL TREAT YOUR FURNITURE LIKE OUR OWN. Their own furniture must be some mess, Lily thought. And then, worse, what would everyone in Rockaway think when they saw the Mollahans arriving for the summer in a truck that was falling apart, an upright piano lashed to the back with rope, and Lily and Gram sitting squashed in the front seat? Lily closed her eyes. Horrible.

At least Gram had forgotten about the report card. Lily went downstairs to watch the two white-haired men in the living room. They were talking to Gram, joking a little, one of them singing, " 'They're either too young or too old,' " while the other was telling Gram that both their sons were in the service and that they were keeping the business going for the duration of the war.

Gram was frowning, watching them hoist up the piano with a bowl of flowers still on top. Lily could see they'd be stuck at the door; the piano wouldn't go through in a million years. Alleluia. And better yet, her report card was on the bottom step of the stairs. Gram wasn't paying attention to it. Lily knew she was worrying about the piano scratching the wall as the men worked on shoving it through the door.

Lily reached down for the report card, backed up the stairs. She could see herself in the truck, Gram suddenly saying, "I never did look at your report card, Lily. Do you know where . . ."

Perfect. Lily wouldn't say a word. Gram had lost the thing herself. Not Lily's fault, certainly not.

Up in her bedroom, she looked around. Her book, *Evangeline*, was still on the dresser. Lily moved the star to the front page and put the blue report card in the back as far away from the star as possible. Her mother would never have cared for report cards.

And ten minutes later, finally, Lily was packed. She picked up the last carton, listening to the perfume bottle clinking into her lipstick samples from Gertz Department Store in Jamaica, FREE TAKE ONE. Lily had taken a bunch, you never knew when stuff like that would come in handy.

She started down the stairs with the carton, and *Evangeline* tucked carefully under her arm. At the other end of the hall was the wrenching sound of wood splitting, the molding hanging loose. Still in the living room, Gram made an angry sound, but one of the men was telling her not to worry, molding was nothing, they could fix it up in a jiffy. "Tell Mr. Mollahan we'll come back next week and . . ."

The piano. They had gotten it through. It stood there in the hall, huge, with round glass stains on the top and two of the keys missing the ivory. And then the men lifted it again and started out the door. Lily followed them, circling around Gram still powdering her nose at the hall mirror.

The piano was in the truck now, with one of the men looping great pieces of rope around it, telling the other one, "I'll stay back here, just to make sure the thing doesn't roll out." He winked at Lily, thinking it was a great joke.

Some joke. Gram came out the door wearing her blue summer hat with the cherries. She climbed up into the passenger seat, leaving a spot next to the window for Lily. "We're off," she told Lily, "at last. I never thought we'd make it this year."

Gram was smiling; she loved Rockaway too. Lily closed her eyes as the truck started off. She didn't want to look at the neighbors, who were waving at them and the piano and the rusty truck, probably thinking they were crazy.

But then they turned the corner, heading for the Belt Parkway, heading for Cross Bay Boulevard, and the bridge, and Lily could feel the excitement of it, the ocean waiting, the sound of it, the roll of it, and it was hers for the whole summer.

She didn't open her eyes when Gram began about the report card. She could feel the vibration of the motor, and hear the man in front singing, " 'They're either too young or too old,' " and Gram humming along. And the next thing she heard was the sound of the tires hitting the planks of the bridge. They were there.

Rockaway . . .

Chapter 3
ROCKAWAY, 1944

*L*ily received three and a half presents for her birthday
that Monday. Two were books, one was a secret, and the
last was a half-eaten candy bar.

Margaret Dillon gave her the candy, a Milky Way. The
end of the wrapper was torn back, and teeth marks dented
the chocolate.

"I stole it," Margaret said. "Stole it for you, and kept
thinking about it, and my mouth watered, and I just
couldn't—"

"—resist," said Lily.

"Right." Margaret grinned. "A tiny bite."

Lily took the Milky Way by the wrapped end and slid it into her pocket. She was dying to wipe her fingers on her skirt, but she couldn't hurt Margaret's feelings.

Lily followed Margaret and her two cats up the bareboard steps to the Dillons' attic. It was almost the only stand-up attic in Rockaway Beach, a perfect place to look out the window and see what was going on all over the place. Most of the other summer houses had tiny crawl spaces, and Gram's house, over on the bay side, didn't even have that. Gram's house was built up over the water on stilts, without an attic, or a cellar, or even a bathroom with a real tub.

"Now, listen." Margaret leaned toward her, the freckles on her nose like four dots of pepper. "I have a pack of things to tell you and they're all secret."

"I won't tell," Lily said, feeling the heat of the attic, dying to take a quick peek out the window, to do a little spying on the beach at the end of the street.

"You have to swear . . . ," Margaret began.

Outside, the July sky was so blue it almost hurt Lily's eyes, and the wind was just right, so the beach would be packed. Spies were probably sitting there under their striped umbrellas checking on the ships that steamed away from the Brooklyn Navy Yard.

Margaret's eyes narrowed. ". . . swear on your aunt Celia's life in Berlin, Germany."

Lily swallowed. She thought of her list of problems: *Number 1: Lies,* and then the second list, the list of solutions. Right up there on top was the promise not to tell a lie ever again, not even a tiny little one, much less one of those gigantic ones about her aunt being an important U.S. spy against the Nazis.

This was the very last one, she told herself, no matter what. She closed her eyes and crossed her heart over her white blouse. "I, Elizabeth Mollahan, promise never to tell your secrets, on my aunt Celia's life."

"And if you tell," Margaret said, "your aunt will probably be caught by the Nazis . . . not my fault . . . and they'll make her tell all the secret war stuff and—"

"She'd never do that. She's the bravest—" Lily snapped her teeth together hard before the rest of the lie came out.

Where had her aunt Celia gotten herself to, anyway? Lily hadn't even seen her since she was about four years old.

"She'll be marched out, put up against a wall, and shot just like in—"

"—*Fair Stood the Wind for France.*" Lily and Margaret had sneaked in to see it at the Cross Bay Theatre three times yesterday.

"Right," said Margaret. "Now here's the first thing I want to tell you. Come on."

Margaret ducked around the side of the chimney with

Lily behind her. Overhead, Lily could hear the drone of one of the trainer planes from the naval base. She'd love to watch it circling over the beach, dipping its wings . . .

"Are you paying attention?" Margaret asked. "Here I am ready to trust you with all my secrets . . ."

Lily sank down next to her, taking one of the cats on her lap. "I'm listening. Of course I'm—"

Margaret reached for a paper bag. "Look." She held it out. Inside were about fourteen candy bars . . . Hershey's, Walnettos, Sugar Daddy lollipops, and even a couple of rolls of assorted LifeSavers.

Lily's eyes widened. Not counting the dusty case in Mrs. Tannenbaum's stationery store, she had never seen so much candy in her life. She reached out to run her fingers over a roll of Necco wafers. Her mouth was watering. She could see four yellow ones in a row, her favorites . . .

"Maybe we could take one thing," Margaret said. "Just one. My mother is saving all this for my brother Eddie in the army. Now that he's a soldier fighting for his country, he gets everything, and I don't even get a sniff of this stuff. She's going to send it all overseas in this heat. The whole thing will be one big melted mess."

Almost without thinking, Lily reached for the Necco wafers and began to rip open the paper.

"You like that?" Margaret asked. "Not me. I'm going to have a nut thing. Something with chocolate."

They sat there, not talking, Lily crunching down on two yellow Necco wafers, feeling the sweetness in her mouth. "I hope Eddie won't mind," she said.

"Listen," Margaret said, "there's enough candy here for the whole army." She stopped. For a moment she looked worried. "D-Day. I wonder if he was there."

Lily had a quick flash of Eddie in her mind, his square front teeth, a little separated, resting gently on his lower lip, his nose red. He always had a cold, was always sniffling even on the hottest day of the summer. What Lily liked best about Eddie was that she could make him laugh. He always knew when she was telling Margaret a story; he never gave her away.

One time she had told Margaret she had almost seen a murder on Cross Bay Boulevard. A car had screeched to a stop in front of Bohack's at closing time, and the Bohack guy wouldn't let the man in. The man said something about being ready to throttle him, whatever that meant exactly, but he had gone away two seconds later. Lily hadn't mentioned the going away part to Margaret, though.

"I think I even heard the police sirens," Eddie had said.

"Yes," Lily hadn't stopped for a breath. "About four police cars. They zeroed right in."

Eddie Dillon with those square teeth, always ready to laugh. Eddie at Normandy beach on D-Day? Everyone had talked about it all through the war . . . the day that the Allies, thousands of Americans and Englishmen, would land in France to fight their way across Europe.

Lily had seen the news at the movies, boats coming close to the shore, the water rough as Rockaway on a stormy morning. The forward flaps of the little square boats had come down, and soldiers had waded through water almost to their waists, while the Germans kept shooting and shooting . . . She shivered.

"What is it?" Margaret asked.

Lily shook her head. "Nothing."

Margaret fished through the candy. "Take one more thing," she said. "I'm going to try a couple of Walnettos next, and maybe just one butterscotch."

Lily finished the Necco wafers and took a butterscotch too. At home Gram would never let her buy butterscotch candies. "They pull the fillings right out of your mouth," she'd say.

"Now the next thing is really secret," Margaret said, her mouth full. "We're moving out of Rockaway until the end of the war. My father has a job in a factory at Willow Run. It's in Detroit, wherever that is, largest factory in the world. Top secret. We're going to lock the house, board up the windows, and off we go. My mother, my father, me, and even the cats." She leaned forward. "He's going to make those Liberator bombers. B-24's."

Margaret had the best luck in the world, Lily thought. But then she thought about the summer without her. "When?"

"Tomorrow," Margaret said. "The next day at the latest."

"But we were going to . . ." Lily closed her mouth around another butterscotch. It wasn't so much that they were going to do anything. But Margaret, who lived at the other end of Queens all winter, had no idea that she was a last-row, last-seat kid in school with terrible marks in everything except reading. Margaret didn't know she told lies every other minute. No, she didn't know any of that. That's what made her such a perfect friend.

"I know we were going to do a ton of stuff," Margaret said, "but this is important, right? My father has to help win the war. And you could link up with those kids in Broad Channel . . ."

Lily stared out the window. She couldn't even begin to think about getting herself over to Broad Channel, walking up and down the streets, looking for friends, trying to act like Shirley Temple, the actress, when she saw a kid her age, trying to smile. *My name is Lily Mollahan, la la, what's yours?* She shuddered, thinking about it.

"Did you hear something?" Margaret asked, raising one hand.

Lily listened a little nervously. It couldn't be Nazis on such a sunny day. Maybe Margaret's mother back from the stores?

Margaret shook her head. "I guess not." She held the box of Walnettos up to her nose and breathed in. "Of course going to Willow Run isn't quite as good as having an aunt a spy."

"No," Lily said.

"Or a cousin a general in the navy."

Lily tried to look modest. She couldn't even remember telling Margaret that.

"I have one more secret. It's another birthday present. It'll make you feel better when I'm gone." Margaret reached under her collar and pulled a key, knotted in a brown shoelace, over her head. "This is for you, the back door key. You can sneak in, come right up to the attic, and write your next five books."

Lily took a breath. This place, hers. She'd be here by herself, nobody knowing, without Gram telling her to stop reading and get herself outside in the fresh air, without the radio blaring war news in back of her. She'd write a wonderful book, never mind the spelling, never mind Sister Eileen.

She took the key, still warm from Margaret's neck, and looped it under her blouse. "This is the best present I've ever had."

"I know it." Margaret glanced at the brown paper bag. "And you got the best candy bar. I love those Milky Ways."

"You're right." Lily reached into her pocket and handed it to Margaret. "Have a bite of this. Have it all."

Margaret thought a moment. "It's only fair. You've got

the attic, an aunt a spy, your father probably going overseas any minute, and you've already written thirteen books."

"Fourteen . . . ," Lily began, another lie, and stopped. "Poppy's not going overseas. He's not going anywhere." She shook her head. "You forgot. He's an engineer. He's important right where he is, working in the city."

Margaret peeled the paper back off the rest of the candy bar. "My father said he probably would go this summer."

Lily scrambled to her feet. "Your father's wrong."

Then she saw Margaret's eyes widen. "Holy mackerel," Margaret said, "it's my mother."

Lily looked over her shoulder. Mrs. Dillon was coming up the attic steps. Lily could see the top of her head first, and then her shoulders.

They scooped the candy back into the bag, Lily trying to swallow the rest of the butterscotch, which was stuck to her back teeth.

And then Mrs. Dillon was right there, standing in front of them, looking as if she would burst into tears. "How could you?" she said, looking at Margaret. "I walked for blocks for that candy, one store after another, this one didn't have peppermints, the other didn't have Hershey's. There's a war on, no candy . . ." Mrs. Dillon looked out the window. "My poor Eddie," she said.

Lily edged her way to the stairs, feeling guilty, feeling horrible. "I think I'd better go home now," she said, using her best manners. "It was very nice of you to have me over."

She rushed down the stairs, and as she let herself out the door, she could hear Mrs. Dillon. "That Mollahan girl is trouble," she was saying. "And you're not one bit better."

Lily stopped to see if Margaret was going to say anything, but she couldn't hear a thing. She dug the last of the butterscotch off her back teeth and headed for Gram's. The summer certainly wasn't starting off very well, not very well at all.

Chapter 4

Gram's house was the last one on the canal. "Where the ocean swoops in to fight with the bay," she always said.

Up on stilts, the house hung over the water. In the living room was a deep, soft couch, a radio on legs, and, this year, the damn piano taking up the whole side wall. In back was a square little kitchen. It had so many pots and pans, and bowls, and dishes, and mixers, and mashers, that there wasn't an inch of room left on the yellow counters. Most of the stuff was dusty. Gram hated to cook.

The two bedrooms were separated from the kitchen by long flowered curtains. One was Gram's, the other was Poppy's.

Lily was glad there wasn't a third bedroom. All summer she slept on the porch that was tacked on the front. She was so close to the water beneath, she could lean over in her bed and watch the silver killies zigzagging along just under the dark surface.

Sometimes she looked up at the Big Dipper, but most of the time, like tonight, she watched the searchlights crisscrossing overhead. She knew the spotters were looking for enemy planes that might come all the way from Germany to bomb New York.

And suppose she was the one to spot a plane and bombs coming down? She thought about it, diving through bombs to rescue the neighbors. She closed her eyes. Germans parachuting into the canal. She'd have to row like crazy, zigzagging away from the bombs, away from the paratroopers. It made her dizzy to think about it.

She listened. Something was going on. Noise. Lights. At Mrs. Orban's, four houses down. Yes, lights. Mrs. Orban hadn't even bothered to pull the blackout curtains, and the Nazis could zero right in with Lily two seconds away.

And right now, a car was driving up on the road side of the Orbans' house. Lily knelt up in bed and leaned against the screen. Never mind that Gram had told her a hundred times she was going to knock the screen out and go headfirst into the water.

"Mr. Orban's Model A Ford," she said aloud. She knew that because she had helped him paint the top half of the headlights black so they couldn't be seen from the sky. The light Mr. Orban had painted had turned out much better than the one she had worked on.

Lily reached for her shorts and sneakers. She'd just get herself down there and find out what was going on. She wasn't one bit sleepy yet, anyway.

Strange that Mr. Orban was using the last drop of his gas. He had sworn he was going to hold on to it until the day when the war was over in Europe. "Then you and I, Lily my love, are going to drive up and down Cross Bay Boulevard," he had said. "We'll honk the horn every inch of the way."

She thought about sneaking out through the kitchen, but Gram would be awake in a flash. Instead she unhooked the screen and pushed it until it swung out.

Noisy, much too noisy. She counted to fifty, then wiggled through the opening and hung on to the window ledge until she felt the piling with her feet. The rowboat was directly underneath. She let go and landed on one of the oars.

For a minute she rocked back and forth holding her leg,

feeling the pain shooting down her shin. Tomorrow she'd have a black-and-blue mark the size of a potato.

The boat was rocking too, water sloshing in over the side. She could hear Mrs. Orban's back door opening, and the sound of voices, but they were too far away for her to know what they were saying.

Lily pulled the thick rope over the hook, setting the boat free. Then she pushed herself along under the porches, moving from piling to piling, not bothering with the oars.

She looked up as she passed slowly under the Colgans', the Graves', the Temples'. Narrow slits of light from the sides of their blackout shades were reflected out onto the water, sliding up and down with the tiny waves.

Under the Orbans' porch, everything was still except for a gentle swish and the boat bumping against the pilings. The voices had stopped.

Lily sat there shivering, wishing she had brought her sweater. She wondered how long she should stay there. If she boosted herself up on the piling, quietly, carefully, she could grab on to the edge of the porch. The Orbans' porch was a plain open one, not like hers, which had been made into a bedroom. She could tiptoe across it and see into the kitchen window. She thought about it for a moment.

Gram said her whole trouble was she didn't think about things long enough. Of course she did. She thought all the time, about writing stories, and about the war, and about coming to Rockaway every summer. And she thought about her mother. Hadn't she brought a star every year to paste in back of her bed so her mother would be there in Rockaway too? Of course, Gram didn't know that. That was private stuff; no one knew, not even Poppy. Especially not Poppy. His face would get that soft look, that sad look.

Lily reached for the dripping rope and looped it over the Orbans' hook. All she needed was for the boat to float away without her. She slid the oars under the seats on one side. One almost broken shin was enough for tonight. Then she pulled herself up, hanging on to the rough floorboards of the porch.

She left a trail of wet sneaker prints going across, but they'd be dry before morning. And then she was under the window, and Mrs. Orban was talking again, talking a blue streak in her high voice, and Mr. Orban was talking too, a rumble of sound.

Lily crouched there, listening, catching bits and pieces. "Budapest . . . so far away," Mrs. Orban was saying, "but never mind . . . safe and sound . . . the beach . . . swimming . . ." Her voice trailed off.

"Maybe you'd like applesauce," Mr. Orban put in. "Or toast . . . margarine on it, though . . . butter's gone . . ."

"Andrassy Street," Mrs. Orban said. "I remember the cobblestones, and Kalocsa's Restaurant . . ."

"How about toast with applesauce on the side?" Mr. Orban asked. "What do you say, Albert?"

Albert? Who was that, now? Lily leaned back against the house to look at her leg. In the light from the window, she could see it was a mess.

Albert wasn't talking, not a word. Lily listened to Mr. Orban complaining that you had to be a genius to make the can opener work, while Mrs. Orban kept going on about the beach.

Then Lily heard her own name, clear as a bell. Lily Mollahan. Albert, whoever he was, was supposed to meet her, and they were going to be friends, Mrs. Orban was saying.

Lily knelt up slowly, so slowly it was as if she were swimming underwater. She gripped the edge of the windowsill with the tips of her fingers, then raised her head just high enough to see inside, and to hear clearly. And what she heard was Albert saying he didn't have time to be friends with any Lily Mollahan, saying her name in a strange, soft way, with an accent. "I have to find Ruth," he said.

What was he doing there, she wondered, sitting at the table directly across from her, a dish of applesauce in front of him, the skinniest kid she had ever seen in her life. His hair was curly and thick, but it looked as if he hadn't combed it in a hundred years. She stared at him, his face down in the shadows. A nice face, she thought, even

27

though he didn't want to be friends. Too bad for him. She didn't want to be friends either.

He was wearing shorts, and his knees were big and knobby under the table, his legs like sticks. Then he looked up. His eyes were blue, the bluest she had ever seen, and he was looking straight into her eyes. He picked up his spoon, a little applesauce dripping off the edge, and, still staring, pointed it at her.

She could feel the heat in her face, and in her neck. Mr. and Mrs. Orban were turning toward the window, trying to see what he was looking at outside. Lily scrambled across the porch on her knees, and down over the edge, hanging on for a second, landing in the boat, grabbing the rope off the hook as fast as she could. She pushed herself back down under the porches so quickly she could hear the water churning up in back of her.

She didn't stop until she was in her bed with the red quilt pulled up to her chin. She lay there thinking about Albert—his blue eyes staring at her—and wondering who Ruth was. She couldn't believe she had been caught like that, sneaking around on the Orbans' porch in the middle of the night.

Chapter 5

*L*ily had been wandering around all of yesterday and today, trying to get another look at Albert. She wore the sailor hat Eddie Dillon had given her last summer, her sunglasses, and a thick layer of Victory Red lipstick from Gertz Department Store, FREE TAKE ONE. Albert wouldn't recognize her in a hundred years.

It didn't make any difference. Once she thought she saw him climbing around on the rock jetties at the beach, and once on Cross Bay Boulevard. But both times he was gone by the time she got close enough for a good look.

Right now it was Friday afternoon, late, and Poppy was finally coming for a weekend. In the rowboat, Lily dipped the oars into the water as quietly as she could. Any minute Gram would be after her to practice the piano, Etude in Something or Other, set the table for dinner, and who knew what else.

"Lil-y."

Too late.

Above her, the screen door opened.

Lily began to row, singing, " 'Mairzy doats . . . ,' " pretending she hadn't heard.

Gram wasn't fooled. "You could set the table, Lily," she called, "get everything ready before your father comes."

"Going to pick him up in the boat right now," Lily said over her shoulder. "Then he won't have to walk around the long way."

"And what about the piano?"

Gram was in love with that piano.

"Did you practice?" Gram began.

"This morning." She hadn't bothered much with the étude, she'd done the C scale twice, two minutes, and that was that. She began to sing again, " 'A kiddley divy too,' " listening for the sound of the door, but it didn't close. Gram was still standing there, waiting for her to turn around and come back.

Lily raised the oars, water plinking off the ends, but Gram didn't say anything.

"Going to get Poppy," she said again.

In back of her the screen door closed.

Lily dipped the oars into the water again, veering toward the railway station, hurrying now, anxious to see him.

The railroad trestle looped across the bay, flat against the water. Lily bent over the oars, wondering what Poppy would tell her about on the way back . . . probably how hot it was in St. Albans and how much he missed her. She smiled to herself, thinking about it.

She saw the smoke from the engine before she spotted the train. A moment later, it pulled into the station, and a knot of people piled out the doors. And there was her father, waving his newspaper at her. She waved back, rowing fast toward the dock, watching the distance narrow, angling around another boat that was coming in to meet the train. Then finally she rammed into the rough wood of the piling. She held the boat steady, stroking, until Poppy untied his shoes, pulled them off, and hopped in.

"Want to row?" she asked, leaning across for his kiss.

He shook his head, smiling, the lines around his eyes crinkling. She reached out to touch them with her fingers.

"Go the long way," he said, "around the trestle."

She knew Gram was waiting, broiling flounder, using the last dot of butter for little round potatoes, but she was so happy to be there with him, she didn't say anything.

She dipped the oars into the water, pulling slowly, evenly, watching him. He tipped his hat back and closed his eyes. "This is my favorite place," he said. "It's home, even though it's only for the summer."

Lily nodded. Tomorrow they'd line up at the deep-sea fishing dock, to climb aboard the *Mary L.* before the sun came up. They'd fish all day, the boat smelling of kerosene and heat.

Tomorrow night, she and Poppy would walk to the Cross Bay Theatre. He loved the movies too. It would be her fourth time for *Fair Stood the Wind for France,* first time paying. Then on Sunday, after Mass, they'd read, finish *Evangeline* or . . .

"I have to tell you . . ." Poppy's eyes were open now, blue with paler flecks of gray, his face suddenly serious.

"The Dillons left for Detroit," she said quickly. "Mr. Dillon's going to be a foreman in a factory in charge of making planes. Top secret, Margaret says."

Poppy grinned. "It won't be top secret for long, not if Margaret knows about it."

Lily swallowed, watching him smile.

He reached out, put his hand on the oars. "I have to go too. I came tonight to tell you."

She didn't look at him. "To a factory like the Dillons? When would we leave?"

She looked out across the water, seeing him shake his head from the corner of her eye.

"The army needs engineers," Poppy said.

For a moment she felt as if she couldn't breathe. "Who's going to take care of me?"

"Gram," he said. "Gram, of course."

Gram. She closed her mouth over the word, didn't want to hear it. She and Gram all alone in St. Albans this winter, the wind rattling around the house.

"Please," she said, but she didn't even know if she had said it aloud.

Poppy put his hand over hers. "Listen. People are being killed just for disagreeing with the Nazis, or being Jewish."

"I'm sick of the war," she said.

"It's going to be over someday," he said, "now that the Allies have landed in France."

She shook her head. "It'll take forever."

Poppy sighed. "There's been nothing but destruction in this war, families separated, villages ruined, cathedrals bombed . . ."

She opened her mouth, trying to think of something to say, something that would change his mind.

"But right behind the armies will be people like me," he said. "The engineers, the builders. We're the ones who'll help put Europe back together again."

"Where will you go? When . . ."

He shook his head. "It could be anywhere. England, maybe, or Germany."

"I won't even know where you are."

"Yes, you will," he said.

Lily shook her head. "Mrs. Colgan doesn't know where her brother is. She said the censors cross everything out in the letters. She can't even guess what country."

Poppy squeezed her hand. "That's true. But I promise, I'll find a way to let you know, somehow."

Gram was calling now. She could hear her voice across the water. "Jerry, Lily, hurry."

"I love you, Lily," Poppy said. "I love you more than Rockaway. More than anything."

Lily edged the boat toward the dock. Gram was outside, her hand cupped over her eyes, watching for them.

"What will Gram say?" Lily asked. "She won't like it. She'll hate it. I know she will."

Poppy moved his hand, held it over Lily's wrist on the oar. "Gram knows."

Lily stared at him. "You told Gram first. You knew about it. Both of you keeping a secret . . . not telling me . . ."

She shook his hand off her wrist, feeling tears hot in her eyes, a terrible burning in her throat, feeling angry enough to burst. She hated him, hated Gram.

She started to row.

"Lily," her father began, then stopped.

She nosed the boat in under the porch, banging hard into the piling. She must have chipped a piece of paint off

34

the boat, a couple of pieces. She didn't care, didn't care about one thing.

Poppy reached out to help her up, but she pulled away from him.

Gram was standing at the edge of the ramp that led to the kitchen, smiling a little, looking anxious at the same time. "You told her? I thought you were going to wait until after—"

"Mind your business," Lily said, and said it again. The words came out of her mouth so fast, they ran together. Then she ran up the path, away from the house. She wanted to go back to the water, but she'd have to pass them. Instead she went along the road, running on the tar, which was gluey from today's sun. She saw Albert and veered away from him, but she knew he had seen her too. He was standing in front of the Orbans' house, watching her cry.

Chapter 6

The next day, as soon as it was light, Lily was out the door, barefoot, heading for Margaret's house. Peeling shutters covered the windows on the bottom floor, winter shutters. She could hear the radio next door, the newscaster talking about the American army caught on the beaches in Normandy: two hundred thousand soldiers waiting to set Paris free. Was that all anyone thought about—news and the war?

Without looking, Lily slipped the key out from under her collar. She didn't bother to pull the shoelace over her head. She leaned forward. The key fit easily into the lock, the door sliding open under her fingers, and she was inside in a moment.

She wandered into the living room. It was darker than the kitchen in there, the winter shutters tighter on the windows. Still, shafts of light fell across the rug, and the couch, and Eddie's picture on the end table.

She picked up the picture, seeing Eddie's smile, his buck teeth, his boots laced up tight, his cap pushed back over his frizzy hair. She thought of Poppy, and how he would look in a uniform.

She set the picture back in exactly the same spot. How strange it seemed without Margaret, or even Mrs. Dillon sitting next to the radio listening to *Portia Faces Life*. Lily went up the attic stairs, listening to the sound of her feet, and pushed up the window.

The waves were high today. No one was on the boardwalk except a gray gull sitting on the railing, its feathers puffed out over its skinny legs. The legs reminded her of someone, but she couldn't think of who it was.

The *Mary L.* was still at the dock, sitting low in the water. If only she'd see Poppy in line with the other fishermen. He'd be balancing the picnic basket and tackle box; he'd have his fishing rod and hers too.

She felt a terrible lump in her throat. He was probably

packed by now, having breakfast, ready to take the morning train back to the city. And she wouldn't be there to say goodbye.

He had told her about the train last night when she had finally gone home. He had sat on the edge of her bed, his weight tilting the mattress down, telling her the war would be over sometime and they'd be right back there in Rockaway with everything just the same.

She hadn't said a word. She had acted as if she didn't care, not one bit.

Now she swallowed hard over the lump in her throat. She wasn't going back. She would stay in the attic all morning, all day, writing a book or something. She wished she could stay there forever.

She took deep breaths of the cool air that was coming in. And, leaning over, she saw Albert. He was alone on the beach, wearing a pale green shirt and shorts. Holding up the shorts was a belt . . . a ridiculous belt that was miles too big for him.

"Ah," she said aloud. That's what the seagull reminded her of. Albert. He had those same skinny legs with fat knees. He was walking back and forth, shading his eyes with his hands, turning toward her.

"Oh no you don't," she said under her breath. She ducked away from the window, walking doubled over to the back of the chimney.

Poor Eddie's candy was gone, bag and all. Only the

Milky Way wrapper was left, over in the corner crumpled in a ball.

Lily looked closer. A piece of paper was lying on the floor. She sank down and picked it up, a note from Margaret.

Don't worry, Lily. I'm coming back. Good luck to your Aunt C in Berlin, Germany. I won't tell anyone.

M.D.

And taped to the bottom was a LifeSaver, a red one, Lily's favorite color.

Lily leaned back against the rough chimney bricks, sucking on the LifeSaver wondering if Poppy's train had left.

She stood up suddenly, so quickly she felt dizzy. Then she was out of the attic, clattering down the stairs, through the hall, through the kitchen, and out the door, listening for the sound of the train. She didn't stop to see whether anyone saw her.

It was too late to get to the station. Instead she ran across the field to the viaduct over the water, trying to find enough breath to get her there ahead of the train. She began to wave as soon as she heard the sound of it on the tracks, even before she saw it. She didn't stop until it was a smudge in the distance, and then gone completely, even though she knew Poppy couldn't have seen her.

Chapter 7

$\mathcal{I}$t was Monday afternoon. Lily put on her sunglasses, her Eddie Dillon sailor hat, stuck a Gertz lipstick in each pocket of her shorts, and her notebook under one arm. It was a beautiful day, a perfect day, and she had something perfect to do.

Spy.

That Albert person had been ducking around all over the place yesterday, here one minute, there the next, always one step ahead of her, one step ahead of the police maybe.

She had thought the whole thing over. Albert could really be a Nazi spy . . . not a chance-in-a-million spy like Mr. Egan, but a real one. She counted it out on her fingers, talking to herself as she marched down the block. One, he had come in the middle of the night; two, he had some kind of foreign spy accent, and three, she couldn't keep track of him.

As soon as she turned the corner, she stopped to put on a slash of Victory Red lipstick. She was getting good at it, not so much on her teeth anymore, or extra around her mouth. At least she hoped not; there were no mirrors on the way to the beach. She smacked her lips, a little sore from all that rubbing off lipstick before she went home every day.

Then she heard footsteps across the street. She looked back. A miracle. It was Albert. She ducked behind the mailbox to watch him. It looked as if he was heading for the beach.

She let him get a half-block ahead of her, up the board-walk steps and down the other side; then she followed along after him. Instead of taking the steps, she scooted underneath the boardwalk and sank back behind the rusty wire fence to see where he went.

He was carrying something, a big wad of stuff. He passed about two inches in front of her, another miracle that he didn't see her, and stopped. What was he up to?

He unrolled the lump, a beach blanket, one of Mrs. Orban's. She'd seen it on the wash line a hundred times, so there wasn't anything much suspicious there. He sat down and lined up a bottle of Coke, a bag of something— sandwiches or a foreign spy radio maybe—and a pad of paper and a pencil. Then he settled himself on the blanket, just sitting there looking out at the water, his bony knees up almost to his chin.

It was a good thing she didn't have anything to do. She could sit there as long as he did. She certainly wasn't going to hang around Gram's house. She was hardly talking to Gram since the night before Poppy left. She took a breath. Don't think about Poppy. Think about Gram instead.

She could see Gram's name, fourth on her problem list. It came after *First: Lies; Second: Daydreaming;* and *Third: Friends, need.* And now maybe she'd cross the whole thing out and move Gram up to number one. It would serve her right.

Gram probably wouldn't care even if she knew. She wasn't talking much to Lily either, mumbling once, ". . . terrible that you didn't come back to say goodbye to your father."

Lily knew it was terrible, she didn't need Gram to tell her that. The last two days she had awakened with a pain in her chest, almost like a woodpecker banging away at her ribs. If only she had gone home on Saturday morning, or even to the railroad station. Just a few minutes would have made all the difference. And now she might not see Poppy for years, she might be grown up and he wouldn't even recognize her.

She had written to him, though, a long "I'm sorry" letter. She had sent it to the address that he had left on her bed. It was a strange address, full of numbers and letters, and didn't even tell where he was.

Suddenly she felt cold there in the shade. She moved her head, finding a shaft of sunlight that came through the boardwalk up above. It was warm on her face. In front of her, a woman went past, humming "The Last Time I Saw Paris."

And Albert wasn't just looking at the water anymore. He was writing something on that pad. What? She could see a ship way out. Maybe he was checking out troop movements. She tried to think what else the spies checked out when she saw them in the movies. She wondered if she could get up a little closer.

Albert's head was bent over his paper, and he was writing fast. Lily crawled around the side of the rusty fence an inch at a time. If he heard her, if he turned around . . .

She pictured herself as an undercover agent. If Albert, Nazi Spy Albert, turned, he'd reach into the bag, pull out his revolver with the silencer. He'd shoot her, of course. Never mind. It was for the good of the country. She'd win a medal.

She couldn't see anything on his paper. His shoulder was in the way. She moved over a bit, and another inch or two toward him, and there, she could see the writing on the lined white paper:

Dere Ont Eva and Onkl Emery,

Strange. A secret code maybe. She frowned, suddenly knowing what it was, feeling the disappointment. A letter, just a letter, not a spy thing at all . . . just that he was the worst speller in the world, worse than even she was. She let out her breath.

He heard her and turned. Good grief. "I lost my, um . . . ," she began, and then she heard the noise.

It was like a mosquito at first, a thin, high sound. It wasn't a mosquito, though, of course not. The noise grew louder, so loud she could feel the boardwalk tremble with it, could feel the vibration in her chest.

A plane was coming in over the water, so low it was just above the waves, its wings tilting. She could see people standing on the beach watching, Mrs. Colgan far down on the beach, looking up, her mouth a perfect round O. And a fat lady with wobbly legs, shading her eyes to see as the plane roared over the beach. It spread a huge, dark shadow, sand flattening under it and spewing up along the sides.

Lily backed against the boardwalk steps, her heart thumping in her chest, her head bursting with the sound of it. Sand was in her mouth and nose, stinging her eyes.

The plane gathered speed, gathered height, was up,

over them and past. And then she realized. It was a trainer plane, only a trainer plane from the navy yard.

But Albert couldn't know that. She could see his face, his blue eyes huge, the pad gone out of his hand, blowing across the beach.

Without thinking, she went toward him, spitting out sand, wiping her eyes on her sleeve. The noise of the plane was fading, and she could see Albert's hands were trembling a little.

She reached out and grabbed his arm. "It's all right," she told him. Then everything was still, except for the waves rolling in on the shore in front of them.

"It's all right," she said again. "It wasn't a Nazi. I saw it." She made a circle with one finger. "The round insignia thing with the star."

He didn't look at her. It almost seemed as if he hadn't seen her as he kept watching the plane, a speck now in the distance.

She stepped back. She could still feel her heart pounding.

"It was a trainer plane." She pointed across the shoreline toward Coney Island. "From the naval base."

He wasn't listening. He followed his paper across the beach, and suddenly she remembered he had caught her spying on him again. Feeling her face redden, knowing she wouldn't go near him for the rest of the summer, she went up the boardwalk steps and started for home.

Chapter 8

Gram was sitting on the couch in the living room when Lily came in. She was listening to *Portia Faces Life*. Lily liked to listen to Portia too.

In fact, she and Margaret had sent away for Portia's picture. They'd written a letter straight to WEAF radio station just before Margaret had left. Margaret said stars like Portia always had pictures of themselves lying around.

Right now on the radio, Portia's husband, Walter, was a

prisoner of war in Germany, and he had just thought of an escape plan. He was going to hide in a small boat. Then when an American ship passed he'd signal it with a flashlight and row out to freedom.

Lily sank down on one end of the couch, as far away from Gram as she could get, to listen.

She could see Gram's hand, soft and plump on the pillows. Gram's wedding ring was a sliver of silver that had made a deep ridge in her finger. "I was skinny until you started school," she had told Lily once, laughing. "Then I started to eat and found out how good food was."

Lily couldn't picture it, couldn't picture Gram skinny, and swimming all the way across Jamaica Bay. Her father had told her Gram had done that. "I watched her when I was small," he had said. "She had a braid to her waist, and she was a seal in the water."

Gram still had the braid, but now it was twisted around in back of her head in a bun. At night, she'd take out the bobby pins, run her fingers through her hair, and brush it.

Gram's hand was moving. Lily watched out of the corner of her eye as the plump fingers walked across the pillows, and Gram's arm came up around her.

Lily was about to shrug her arm away, about to get up, but it felt so good to be sitting there in that circle that she moved closer. A moment later, she was crying, and she didn't even try to stop.

"I know," Gram said.

Lily shook her head. "No, you don't."

Gram touched her sleeve, making tiny pleats in the cotton with her fingers.

"We were going to go fishing," Lily said, "and to the movies. We were going to do everything."

"Your father said exactly the same thing," Gram said.

Lily looked up. "Really?"

Gram nodded. "Your eyes will be red."

She shook her head. "I don't care."

"Yes, you will," Gram said. "We're going out to dinner."

"Trixie's Restaurant?"

"Of course not. There's a war on and not a penny to spare for such foolish—" Gram broke off. "We're going to the Orbans'."

Lily sat up straight. She could feel her mouth suddenly go dry. "I'm not—"

"Mr. Orban said you did a magnificent job on his headlight."

"I don't—"

"There's a surprise for you, Mrs. Orban said."

Lily bit her lip. Some surprise. As if she couldn't guess. Albert. Lily moved back to her end of the couch. She was definitely not going to the Orbans' house, not in a million skillion years.

"I'm not . . . ," Lily began again, and stopped. She always loved to go to the Orbans' for dinner. Sometimes there was a flounder Mr. Orban had caught that morning, with corn on the cob, and a cake with jelly icing on top.

How could she say she didn't want to go, that she knew about Albert? And worse, that he knew about her. Gram wouldn't take no for an answer. Never.

Gram was up from the couch now. "We'll have to see what happens to Walter tomorrow," she said. "They're certainly stretching this out."

Lily followed her into the bathroom and watched as Gram opened her compact and took out her powder puff.

Lily leaned forward to look in the mirror. Her eyes were red, and so was her nose.

"Here." Gram ran a washcloth under the tap. "Nice and cool." She held it up to Lily's eyes. "Better in a minute, wait and see."

Gram was right. Lily held her head back and felt the coolness of the cloth on her eyes and her cheeks. In back of her, she could hear the news. An American general had told reporters he needed only three hours of good weather and the army could break out of Normandy and start across France.

Strange, Lily thought, in France the weather was gray and cloudy, and the Americans were caught on a beach that was wet and cold. Here in Rockaway, it was beautiful.

She checked the mirror again. No one would guess she'd been crying.

Gram took her powder puff and waved it over Lily's nose. "I think I hear the church bells. We're supposed to be there at six. Come on."

Lily walked out behind her, taking the smallest steps she possibly could. She dreaded having to meet Albert, actually meet him at last. She wouldn't say a word to him. She'd talk to Mr. and Mrs. Orban and not even look at him.

Mrs. Orban was waiting at the door, excited, smiling. "Have I got a surprise for you," she said.

And behind her was Albert. Albert, with that mop of dark hair and blue eyes. She took a quick look at him after all. He was looking at her too. His mouth opened. "You are Lily?"

"Of course she's Lily," Mrs. Orban said.

Lily raised one eyebrow and put on her "Too bad for you, Sister Eileen" face. Usually she was good at that, but halfway into the face, her eyes slid away because for the quickest second it looked as if Albert was going to laugh.

When she looked back, he was tapping his lip, looking at her, his own eyebrows raised. What was that all about? she wondered. Albert was crazy.

But then Mr. Orban was leading them to the table, his hand on Lily's back, smiling. "Sit here next to me," he told Gram. "And Lily, my love, across from Albert, my nephew. Albert's here from my brother Emery's in Canada to spend the summer."

"From Hungary," Mrs. Orban said at the same time. "To be safe from the war."

Albert looked up. He spoke to Gram, though, not even glancing at Lily. "From Budapest, two years ago." The words sounded different on his tongue, soft, almost musical.

Mrs. Orban shook her head. "It was a long trip for Albert. Through Austria and Switzerland, across the mountains to France, then a ship . . ." She stopped for a breath.

"With Ruth," Albert said.

Mrs. Orban's face suddenly looked different, older, sad. "His eight-year-old sister was sick," she told them. "She's caught in France."

Albert made a sound, said something.

Lily took a quick look, but he was smearing margarine over a slice of bread, looking down. And then Mr. Orban began to talk quickly, and so did Gram, and Lily bent over her plate to bone the fish and begin on the corn. She was starving.

Albert must have been starving too. He bent over his own plate; his hand made a fist around his fork. He ate fast, taking huge bites, shoveling it in.

Gram would have had a fit if she had done that.

He raised his head, and immediately she looked past him, toward the lemon cake on the counter, and beyond to the window. Outside, pairs of socks were hanging on the porch railing. The water was flat and slick with the sun slanting over it.

"Isn't this perfect," Mrs. Orban said. "Just as Margaret leaves, Albert comes. You'll have someone to fish with all summer, Lily."

Gram was staring at her. Lily could feel her eyes. Gram thought she knew what Lily was thinking, thought Lily wouldn't go to the beach with any boy, fish with him, go to the Cross Bay Theatre . . .

What Gram didn't know was that it was probably the other way around.

"Yes," said Gram. "It's perfect. Isn't it, Lily?"

She didn't look at Gram. She took a chunk of corn off the cob, with a bite almost as big as Albert's. She certainly couldn't answer them with her mouth full.

Albert had finished his fish and corn and was into the peas now. Mounds of peas were falling off the edge of his fork. And suddenly he looked up and saw her watching him. He *was* laughing, bringing his hand up to his mouth. And just as suddenly, she knew what he was doing. He was reminding her of the lipstick, Gertz Department Store, FREE TAKE ONE. Good grief.

It was a good thing Mrs. Orban was talking, otherwise Lily might just have jumped up to race out of there and never come back. But what was Mrs. Orban saying? "Albert doesn't know the ocean. He doesn't know how to swim."

"And Lily," Mr. Orban said, "swims like a mermaid."

"She'll teach you, Albert," Mrs. Orban said. "No one swims the way Lily does."

Teach him to swim—she couldn't believe it.

"Except her grandmother," said Mr. Orban.

Gram laughed. "I haven't put my foot in the water since I taught Lily to swim."

Lily remembered that, remembered paddling around in the water, listening as Gram held her feet lightly, pointing her big toes toward each other, angling her hands so the sides of her index fingers slid into the water first. "Everything makes a difference," Gram had said.

And one Friday night, they had showed her father. No life vest anymore, and by that time Lily could dive. She went off the side of the porch, her toes digging into the railing for an instant, then pushing up, arms stretched, head down. She slid underneath smoothly with the sound of the water in her ears, the taste of it on her tongue, up then, and swimming in front of the houses easily, almost as easily as she could walk.

Moments later, she had climbed back up. Her father had wrapped her in a huge towel, hugging her and telling her how proud her mother would have been.

And now Gram was telling the Orbans about Poppy. "I hope he's still at Fort Dix," she said. In back of them the teakettle was whistling. Gram's face was sad. "He'll go to Europe soon, any day. Maybe he's gone already. I hope it isn't Germany."

Lily stuffed her mouth with bread. She wanted to stuff her ears too. She didn't want Gram to talk about it. She didn't want to think about it.

Then Mrs. Orban passed them slices of lemon cake,

apologizing because it was made with margarine and not butter, and Albert began to eat again, two pieces, and then a third. He didn't look at Lily again, and she sat there thinking about him laughing at her, and wondering about his sister, Ruth, and trying to pretend she didn't notice he was there, until they were finished and it was time to go home.

Chapter 9

Thursday. She had been ducking away from Albert for almost a week. It was just the opposite now. Everywhere she went, she saw Albert. Ahead of her, in back of her, even coming out of Sherman's Bakery.

But right now, she had other things to think about. A letter from her father. They had received only a quick postcard: *Arrived safely. Miss you terribly. We'll be fishing this time next year. Letter follows. Best love, Poppy.* Maybe today there'd be a real letter. She could see it in her mind, tissue thin with a red, white, and blue border, exactly the same as the letters Eddie Dillon sent home.

"If you could stop dreaming and finish your breakfast," Gram said.

Lily picked up her spoon. She could see something else too. Gram would be leaning over her shoulder, reading the letter, her lips moving slightly, reading even faster than she could.

Lily ate her cereal without looking once into the bowl. Bits of cream were floating around in the milk, white things looking like tiny fish. She could almost feel them on her teeth.

She shuddered. The white things were floating around inside her now. She went out to the porch and leaned on the screen. The water was swollen this morning, the tide high.

She knew exactly what she'd do. She'd hang around on Cross Bay Boulevard, maybe stop at Sherman's Bakery for a roll or a cookie. She'd grab the mailman before he even got around to her grandmother on the bay side.

If only he'd give her the letter.

She reached under her bed for her pad and pencil and the tan purse with the money she had saved all winter.

"Going to Sherman's," she told Gram's back at the kitchen sink.

Gram made a tiny breathing sound, a "no" sound, but before she could say she shouldn't waste her money on cookies that tasted like cardboard, Lily began, "My money. My Christmas, snow-shoveling, allowance-saving money."

Gram's voice rose. "Then don't forget sunburn lotion. You'll have blisters on your nose."

Lily didn't wait to hear the rest. She was out the door and up the road. Already it was hot, the tar shimmering in the haze, the sound of the cicadas beginning. "Listen," Poppy would say, "it's the sound of summer."

She wondered when she'd see him again. The days stretched out in front of her like long gray sheets on a wash line. Summer would be over, and fall . . .

Lily passed the As Good As New Shoppe on the corner. Everything in the window was just the same, the old coat and dusty straw hat, certainly not looking as good as new, the flute and violin in back, and the stuffed dog that looked as if it would fall over any second.

Sherman's Bakery was at the near end of Cross Bay Boulevard. It was dim and dusty, and Lily could see through the screen that Mrs. Sherman hadn't gotten around to baking yet. The trays were almost empty. A strawberry-pink birthday cake stood on one shelf and a plate of pale sugar cookies on another. The cookies had jelly in the middle, but the jelly would be hard by now, the juice drained out overnight.

Lily stood there, hand on the screen door, squinting in the sun. The mailman was halfway up the next block. She could see him plodding along across the street.

She took a step, but Mrs. Sherman, hands floury, came

out from the back and spotted her. "Lily," she said. "My first customer today."

Lily pulled open the door and went inside, glancing up at the poster over the glass counter: LOOSE LIPS SINK SHIPS.

"Not much left," Mrs. Sherman said. "Sticky buns later, but try those jelly cookies for now."

Lily looked down at the cookies. Up close they looked worse, shrunken and dry. She wondered which way the mailman was going. Toward the bay? Back along the boulevard?

"Can't get much butter with the war on, you know," Mrs. Sherman began, leaning against the counter.

Lily nodded. If the mailman went toward the bay, he'd turn before the bakery. She'd miss him.

"I'll take a cookie," Lily said. "Sure."

"The egg man went into the service," Mrs. Sherman said. "I don't know how I'm going to get eggs now, or cheese."

"My grandmother said I have to be right home. I have to stop for her medicine."

"Sick? Your grandmother's sick?"

The next thing she knew, Mrs. Sherman would be on her way to Gram's with her dried-up cookies. "Uh . . . no. It's my aunt Celia. In Europe."

Mrs. Sherman shook her head, clucking a little. "What's the matter?"

She'd never get out of there. She took a step back, trying to think. She remembered the news awhile back:

battles in Russia, with snow and biting cold. "Frostbite," she said.

Mrs. Sherman raised one eyebrow. "In July?"

Lily shook her head. "I don't know. I really—"

Mrs. Sherman sighed. "It's the war. No one knows what's going on." She reached for a bag. "Two cookies. Two for the price of one."

"Thanks," Lily said. If she ran maybe she could cut the mailman off. She counted pennies out on the counter, reached for the bag, then banged out the screen door.

He was there, crossing the street, still on the boulevard. A miracle.

"Hey," she called. "Wait up."

He didn't turn around. He stopped to stuff a paper into the slot at the restaurant, then went next door to the dry cleaner. By the time she caught up with him, she could feel perspiration streaking down her back.

"I need my mail," she told his sack, not looking at his face.

He'd never even give her the movie advertisement. He shook his head. "I've told you. I have to deliver to your grandmother's house. Can't be dropping her mail all over the place. She'd carry on and—"

"My mail," Lily said. "My own mail."

Inside the sack was her letter, written in her father's handwriting. It would start with "Sweetheart," or "Dear Lily Billy."

"My father," she said in a voice she could hardly hear

herself, "is in the service. The Secret Service." She stopped, trying to think how to convince him. "He told me to be sure to get the mail first. He—"

The mailman looked up. "Jerry went overseas?"

The letter was there, so close she could reach out and take it. She hated the mailman.

"You know you're not supposed to ask," she said. "You saw the poster in Mrs. Sherman's, 'Loose Lips Sink Ships.' Spies could be walking up and down Cross Bay Boulevard, and my father, who's on a ship right now . . ."

She could feel her lips trembling even though she didn't know if her father was on a ship, or still in New Jersey at Fort Dix, perfectly safe.

The mailman shifted the leather strap on his shoulder. "Don't cry, Lily. Let me take a look. Let me just see . . ."

She stood there waiting as he went through dozens of envelopes, it seemed, stacks of papers. He kept shaking his head. Then at last he plucked a letter out of the sack.

She breathed in, and could really feel the tears now.

"It's not from your father," he said.

Then she could see it too. A small white envelope, filthy, MISS LILY MOLLAHAN, in pencil.

Margaret. Only Margaret.

"Listen, Lily," he said. "There'll be a letter tomorrow. Betcha. You'll come right down here to Cross Bay . . ."

She stared at the sidewalk, at a crack running along it, a hill of ants bustling. "He's very busy," she said.

"I know," he said. "He's a great guy."

Lily took the letter from him, dug it into her shorts pocket. "I'll see you tomorrow, then," she said.

"You can count on it."

She headed for the fishing dock, looking back once to wave to him. It was a hot walk along Cross Bay Boulevard, but worth it. The fishing boats would be long gone now on a weekday, out since early this morning. She'd have the wharf to herself, with only a fisherman or two trying for fluke.

She ran the last bit, seeing the weathered dock in front of her, the flag flapping wildly on the pole, and best of all, no one there, not a soul. She took a deep breath, smelling the sea, and kerosene from the boats, and sat on a bench halfway down to read Margaret's letter. But before she even got to take it out of her pocket, she could see someone on the beach path. No, two people. Her luck.

She shaded her eyes. One was coming on a bicycle, wobbling along, a basket in front, and the other, a good way in back of him, seemed to be . . . She sat up straighter. Yes, it was Albert running down the road after him. He stopped once, and darted into the reeds, as the bicycle rider looked over his shoulder. What was Albert up to, anyway?

The rider slowed as he neared the dock. It was probably a fisherman who would talk and talk, and she'd never get one minute's peace, when the person she really wanted to talk to was Albert.

She slid off the bench, leaning against the side. If he

didn't see her, maybe he'd go all the way to the far end on that bicycle and pass her right by.

He didn't, though. She could hear him swinging off the bike, the sound of metal as he rested it against a bench farther down, a splash as he tossed something into the water, and as she peered around the side of the bench, he was on his way again, and Albert was running toward her, waving his arms, shouting.

Chapter 10

*L*ily gathered herself to her feet, looking first at Albert, whose feet were pounding along the wooden pier, and then at the back of the man on the bicycle. No, it was a boy, a teenager. His head was down, bent over the handlebars, his feet pedaling faster, picking up speed as he disappeared into one of the narrow lanes that snaked through the reeds.

Albert was in front of her now, almost babbling as he pointed down into the clear green water. She took a step toward the edge, looking down too. She saw threads of seagrass floating under the surface, and then the bulging bag, almost out of sight, as it sank to the bottom.

"It is a cot," Albert said. "A cot."

She shook her head. "It's too small for a . . ." She drew in her breath. A cat. He meant a cat. She was in the water in an instant, rolling over the side instead of diving, not sure of the depth. It was over her head, much deeper than she would have guessed, maybe seven or eight feet. The water bubbled above her, sunlit at first, and then darker. She turned, and kicked with her feet, her arms out, reaching, reaching . . .

And felt the edge of it, the paper bag shredding away in her fingers. Then, a miracle, the kitten was in her hands.

She kicked up with it, and broke the surface. It was still, unmoving, a sodden reddish mass, as Albert, hanging half off the pier, took it from her.

She swam around to the steps the fisherman used to clean their catch, and pulled herself up.

Albert was standing in the middle of the dock now, wrapping the kitten in the edge of his shirt. She moved toward him, her clothes heavy and dripping, her sneakers filled with so much water it was hard to move. "Don't let her lie still," she said. "Keep her moving."

When she reached him, she grabbed his wrist, shaking his hands, and the cat with them. "More," she told him. She dug the cat out of the end of his shirt and kneaded

64

the fur, holding her head down, until at last she coughed and sneezed.

"She is alive," Albert said. They looked at each other, smiling. How blue his eyes are, she thought, and when he smiled she really liked his face. He looked like another person, almost like a friend.

But he smiled for only a moment. He took the cat from her, rubbing her fur with his shirt, drying it, and looking around. "That boy," he said. "I saw him put the cat in the bag—" He broke off. "I have to make her warm," he said. "I have to dry her."

She nodded. Gram would probably never let her keep a cat, and Mrs. Orban had never had a pet that she knew about. If only Mrs. Dillon were still there.

Margaret's house, she thought. "I know," she told Albert. "I'll show you."

It took ten minutes to get back to Margaret's house. They walked slowly, stopping every few minutes to make sure the cat was breathing. She was curled into a ball, still damp, under Albert's shirt.

Lily led the way around the back. "I know it looks as if no one lives here," she said, "but I have the key, and it really isn't trespassing."

"Trespassing?" He said it after her as if the word had a million *s*'s. "Funny word."

"It means—" she began, and broke off. How could she explain? Besides, they had to be quiet. She held one finger up to her mouth and reached for the key around her neck. She pulled him inside and shut the door quickly behind them.

"Why?" he asked, whispering.

She raised her shoulders, thinking about how to tell him. "It's the war," she began. "The people are gone now."

She saw his eyes, blue in the dim light, sad maybe, or frightened. "Like Budapest," he said.

Lily shook her head a little. "Margaret . . . that's the girl, said I could. Gave me the key. I'm being careful."

She looked at the winter shutters tight over the windows, and breathed in, trying not to cry over the cat, or her father, or Margaret's being gone.

"Hot," Albert said.

Lily shook her head, and then she realized how wet she was, the ends of her hair still dripping.

Albert was frowning. "She is too little for food," he said slowly. "She needs milk," and, even more slowly, "She needs her mother."

Lily nodded, a quick flash in her mind of the stars on her ceiling and her own mother. Then she sat back on her heels. Albert was right. The kitten needed milk. She thought about going for it. She'd have to walk all the way to the bay side and sneak past Gram to take a bottle out of the refrigerator.

No. The tan purse. She could run down to Milton at the grocery store. She slapped her pocket. The purse was gone. Of course, it was in the water. All the money she had saved for all the cookies this summer, and the movies, and it was gone. All those months of saving. But Margaret's letter was still in her pocket. She could feel it, almost as wet as the cat. How could she ever read it? She took it out slowly, carefully, and spread it on the counter to dry.

"I will get milk." Albert reached for the back door. "Do not worry," he said, but it sounded like *werry*.

He was as careful as she would have been, opening the door less than an inch, peering out, then pushing it all the way. A moment later, the door closed gently, and he was gone.

Where was he going? To Mrs. Orban's? To Milton's? He had certainly learned to find his way around quickly.

The cat mewed. On the kitchen floor she was a shadow, so puny she could be only a few weeks old. Poor little thing. Lily could have cried looking at her. She scooped her up, her face a striped pansy, her ears tiny tags of orange. "Coming," Lily said, "milk is coming. Don't *werry*."

She wandered down the hall with the cat in her arms, running her hand over her back, feeling the knobs of her bony spine. The first door was to Eddie's bedroom. She pushed it open with one finger. It was a little lighter in there, the shutters not as tight against the windows.

She remembered when they were about seven, she and Margaret had sneaked in to steal enough money for a sticky bun each at Mrs. Sherman's. Eddie had caught them, and Margaret, fresh as paint Gram would say, told him what they were doing. He had dug into his pocket for a dime and tossed it toward Lily in a silvery arc.

She had reached out, and somehow it had landed in her outstretched hands. She remembered Eddie smiling, his teeth over his bottom lip, his eyes crinkling. "Nice catch."

It was hot in the bedroom, stifling. She had to get out of there. She went back into the kitchen, feeling the flutter of the kitten's heartbeat.

Margaret's letter. She went over to the counter and angled it so a shaft of light ran across the envelope from end to end. She ran her finger lightly over the mess of Margaret's handwriting, the return address, DETROIT, MICHIGAN. And even though it had been in the water, Lily could still see a smear of chocolate on the flap. One more candy bar that would never get to Eddie in Europe.

She sank down on the floor with the letter, the kitten in her lap. The envelope opened easily and the letter came out, damp but still readable.

Dear Lily,

There is no ocean here at Willow Run, no paint on the houses. They go together in a row and you can hear people talking and fighting and even going to the bathroom. The houses were just slapped up because thousands of people have come here to make the bombers. My father took me in to see. The factory is a mile long. Everyone just makes one little piece that they fit together until the B-24 is finished. My father says they build a bomber every 103 minutes. I hate the whole thing. How is the attic? Did you find the red candy?

Margaret

Lily shifted on the floor, peeling her sweaty legs off the linoleum, thinking about Margaret so far away. Margaret without an ocean, without Rockaway. She wondered what Margaret would think about Albert.

Lily leaned over the kitten. "Albert likes cats," she said. "That's something."

Then he was back, a milk bottle in his hands, enough milk for ten cats the size of this one.

"Now." Lily put the cat back on the counter and took the bottle from Albert. She ran her finger under the paper top, popping it up. She tried not to look at the yellow cream just underneath. She'd gag if she saw it. She had to dig it out, though. It might be too thick for the kitten to swallow.

She opened a kitchen drawer, found a spoon, and skimmed off the cream, swallowing hard. She dropped it, spoon and all, into the sink.

"What are you doing?" He took the spoon and sucked at the cream that was left.

She began to gag.

"What is the matter?" He turned the spoon over and ran his tongue over the back.

"Nothing." She handed him the bottle and let him take the last of the cream. A little stayed on his lower lip, a small yellow fish.

She was going to vomit right now. "Wipe your mouth," she told him. She breathed in as he ran the back of his arm over his face, trying to think about chocolate, red LifeSavers, and cookies with jelly in the middle.

"My sister, Ruth, loves cream," he said.

Lily looked up, but the cat was standing on the countertop, one paw out, ready to sail into the air.

"Watch out," she said, and he dived for the kitten and caught her. Then Lily rummaged around for a small round bowl and poured in some of the milk.

For a moment the kitten didn't seem to notice the bowl in front of her. Then at last she turned her head and began to lap at it with her rough little tongue. They watched her until she sat back and her blue-green eyes began to close, and they could hear her begin to purr.

"What are we going to do with her?" Lily asked. "I don't think Gram . . ."

Albert was nodding, looking down at the cat. "Could we keep her here?"

Lily had thought of that too. Mrs. Dillon loved cats. She'd hate it that someone had tried to drown a kitten.

"I have the key," she said, almost to herself.

"If you will lend it to me," he said, "I will feed the cat myself. You don't have to bother. I will be very careful."

"There's a place in the back," she said, "under the edge of the steps. The Dillons left their key there sometimes. I guess . . ." She felt so disappointed, she could hardly finish. He didn't want to be friends. He could have said *We can feed her together*, or even *We can take turns*.

Albert patted the cat's head gently, then took a towel that was still looped over a hook. He made it into a little bed in the corner. There were newspapers there too, and he tore them into strips for the cat's litter, as Lily watched.

She wanted to say, "It's my cat too." She wanted to say, "I was the one who saved her." She didn't, though.

When Albert was finished, she opened the door and, knowing he was watching, went to the back to wedge the key behind the rock.

She started for home without saying goodbye. It was lunchtime anyway. Never mind that Albert didn't want to be friends. After lunch she'd take her library book, *The Three Musketeers*, out in the boat with a pillow . . . the musketeers, who were in France like Albert's sister. Yes, that's what she'd do. Too bad about being friends. She'd read for the rest of the afternoon.

Chapter 11

The church bells were ringing. Six o'clock on a Wednesday night, the end of July. Everyone was gathering up pails and wet towels, and pulling umbrellas across the beach. She couldn't wait until the last family dragged itself off the boardwalk toward the Cross Bay buses. She couldn't wait until the beach belonged to her.

Gram had packed her a supper, Spam on a roll with a tomato from Mrs. Colgan's Victory garden, three or four celery sticks, and a bottle of orange juice.

Lily sat as close to the water as she could get without getting soaked. The tide was high. The waves washed in, then sucked everything back out, shells, and sand, and bits of seaweed. She thought about listening to *Portia Faces Life* with Gram this afternoon. Walter was in a rowboat now, waiting to find an American ship to pick him up. Lily looked out at the water, thinking about Poppy. He'd be on a ship one of these days, maybe even today, crossing the Atlantic, passing Rockaway. She shaded her eyes, watching a lone swimmer in the surf.

She sat up straight. Who was that?

Albert.

He wasn't out far. He was swimming along in a line next to the beach.

He wasn't swimming, though. He pulled himself to his feet, then threw himself down to take a couple of strokes before disappearing under the water. A moment later he was up, sputtering, to start the whole thing over. If a lifeguard had been on the beach, he'd have been out after Albert in two seconds.

Lily stood up. Albert was trying to teach himself how to swim.

He wasn't paying one bit of attention to the water. He wasn't trying to be part of it, to float along with it. He was fighting it, arms slapping, head sticking up like a tennis ball.

She wouldn't be able to eat her Spam in peace; she'd have to watch him every minute.

Albert was going to kill himself.

Yes, there it was, a giant of a wave. She could see it swelling, way out but moving toward him, picking up speed.

She looked toward Albert. Under. Tennis ball head shooting up. An arm out over his head, fingers wide apart.

She stood up, trying to see how much time he had. She cupped her hands over her mouth, shouting. He couldn't hear her, probably couldn't see her.

She took a step toward him. Then she was running, throwing herself into the icy coldness, slicing into the water, swimming diagonally.

Of course she was too late. The wave curled up high, and she was in the wrong position, just where it arched. It smashed into her, dragging her down, scraping her along the sand. She couldn't get her breath. The water was in her mouth, her throat, her nose.

And then she was out of it, coughing up water, arms and legs scratched, lying on foamy sand.

The last time she had done that she was six years old. Poppy had caught her up in his arms and carried her back to the blanket. He had fed her tiny squares of egg salad crunchy with celery.

She looked up to see feet. Skinny Albert feet. Bony Albert legs with black-and-blue marks and grains of sand.

She had forgotten all about him.

She leaned on her hands to push herself up, then scrambled to her feet.

Albert reached out. "I thought you were such a good swimmer," he said.

As soon as she stopped coughing she was going to drown him herself. She was going to take him by his skinny neck and throw him right back.

She went back to the blanket and sat on the edge, wiping her face with her hands. Her nose and throat burned. She remembered the bottle of orange juice and reached for it. She knew he had followed her to the blanket, but she didn't look up.

She wanted to say she could swim better than anyone she knew. Hadn't she saved the cat? But she wanted to say more, that the ocean belonged to her, that all winter at home in St. Albans she thought about it moving and rolling and waiting for her to come back.

"How is the cat?" she said, knowing very well how the cat was. She had spied on Albert going in and out of the house for the last few days. She had let herself in when he was gone. The cat had fluffed up, a soft orange and white. He kept her bed and litter box clean, and the kitchen too.

"The cat is good," he said. He was sitting on the other end of the blanket now, dripping. She didn't know how he had gotten there. He pointed. "Do you see?"

The end of the jetty, a gray triangular rock. She nodded. "Yes."

"If you drew a line straight out, all the way . . ."

"Europe," she said.

He nodded. "Europe."

"Want some juice?" she asked, not looking at him.

He shook his head.

She took a deep swallow of the juice, feeling it soothe her throat, watching a curl of smoke out on the horizon.

"A ship," Albert said, "going to Europe."

"No." She shaded her eyes. "It's a cutter. Coast Guard, patrolling." It felt good to let him know she knew something, knew more than he did.

She took another sip from the bottle.

"My aunt said you can see the ships from here."

"They form a convoy way out," she said, and pointed. "But some of them come from Brooklyn. The destroyers, the carriers, sometimes the tankers. You can see them at night if you watch long enough."

"Going to Europe," Albert said.

She nodded. "Going to win the war for us, going to blast the Nazis right out of the water."

"And your father is going . . ."

Later, when she thought about it, she couldn't imagine saying what she had, it was just that she had been thinking of *Portia Faces Life*, and Poppy crossing out there almost in front of her, and Albert saying, "I thought you were such a good swimmer."

"I'm going too," was what she said. "At night. I'm going to row right out, and swim the last bit. I'll have a rubber bag with dry clothes." It sounded wonderful, and she could see he was listening. He wasn't thinking of her as a silly kid, wearing Gertz lipstick, spying around. "I'm going to take a ship to my father, no one will stop to take me back to Brooklyn, there's a war on, you know . . ." Talking and talking, making up lies as she went along, and Albert, leaning forward . . .

"You could do that?" he asked.

"Of course." She stared at the cutter angling its way west toward Brooklyn until all she could see was a curl of smoke on the horizon. And then, just for a moment, it almost seemed possible. She could see herself reaching the troop ship, climbing aboard, and sailing to Europe to find Poppy.

"And you can see those ships at night?" He took a breath. "Would you take me out to see them? Would you take me out tonight?"

She put the empty bottle back in her bag and started to roll up her towel. "All right," she said, not quite looking at him.

He stood up. "I am going to the house. I will feed my cat. You will come to my porch at eleven?"

He started across the sand, not waiting for an answer.

She sat there a minute longer, her heart pounding, thinking that this was truly the worst lie she had ever told.

Chapter 12

They couldn't watch for ships that night after all. Mr. Colgan had borrowed Gram's rowboat for night crabbing, and Mr. Orban was caulking the bottom of his.

"Want to go to the movie instead?" Lily asked Albert when she caught up with him on the Orbans' porch.

"Well . . ."

"We won't stay for the whole thing," she told him. "We'll just sneak in and watch until eight-thirty, a little *Eyes and Ears of the World News*, and . . ." She tried to remember the newest movie at the Cross Bay. She had seen two minutes of it the other day before the matron had caught her and marched her outside, blinking, into the sunshine.

"How much does it cost?" he asked.

"Not a cent. I told you, we're sneaking in." She could see he looked worried. "Unless you're afraid."

"I am not afraid of anything."

"Well, then." *Action in the North Atlantic* was the name of the movie. It was about the troop ships crossing the ocean, and German submarines following along . . .

She shivered a little, thinking about those ships. Mrs. Sherman had just pinned up another poster over a pile of raisin rings. SOMEONE TALKED, it said in big red letters on top, and underneath was a ship sinking so you saw only the bow, and sailors trying to swim away in waves that were high as mountains.

Lily tried not to think about it. Instead, she walked down the street in front of Albert. They turned in at the alley on one side of the Cross Bay Theatre. The alley was filled with itchy weeds that smelled. She could see Albert lifting his skinny legs as high as he could, but she just rushed right through the weeds and around to the back.

"It's hot as a poker in the balcony," she told him. "They always leave the door open up there."

Albert stopped when he saw the fire escape stairs they'd have to climb.

"Don't be silly," she said, knowing what he was thinking. "Don't look down."

"It must be two stories," he said. "You can fall right through those steps, and it looks as if the steps will pull off the side of the wall."

"Three stories," she said, daring him.

"I am not afraid," he said. "I am just telling you."

She started to climb without answering. She had done this every summer since she was six, up those stairs a thousand times. The stairs were rickety, she had to admit. And the screws holding them to the wall looked rusty as anything. Wouldn't you think the guy who owned the movie would polish things up once in a while?

She looked back over her shoulder at Albert. He was holding on to the railing for dear life, as Gram would say, stopping each second to close his eyes and take a breath.

"Race you to the top," she said.

He opened his eyes. "Sure."

She grinned. He was a tough kid, that Albert.

The balcony door was opened just wide enough for them to crawl through. She sank down on the top step next to the door to watch, with Albert sliding in next to her, breathless. "That was so simple," he said.

She leaned over. "We made it just in time for Bugs Bunny."

He grinned back. "What's up, Doc?" he said.

She started to laugh.

"What?" he asked.

"It's your voice. It sounds so . . . so . . ."

"Hungarian," he said. "It is a Hungarian Bugs Bunny."

She liked the way he laughed, the way he talked. She kept smiling to herself as they leaned back against the step to watch Bugs Bunny chomping on a carrot, falling off a cliff. They had a perfect spot. In fact, they had the whole balcony to themselves. Not one person was up there.

If they had paid, if Poppy had been with her, she would have been able to go downstairs to the candy stand and buy a cup of popcorn, or some peanut chews. If she tried it now—that is, if she'd still had her tan purse with money—the matron with her flashlight would be right there to pounce on her.

And then it was time for the picture. Words . . . music . . . a destroyer being blown up in the water. The noise of it was deafening. Explosions were going on all over the place.

Lily sat there for a while. She watched one of the ships sink and the sailors trying to hold on to little pieces of wood, or to swim away, just like the poster in Mrs. Sherman's bakery.

And she thought of Poppy. They had heard from him again, but only a postcard. She had missed the mailman that day, and the card had slid into the slot in the door, and it had been there all morning until Gram had spotted it. *Never so tired. Never worked so hard, to be ready to go overseas. Thinking of you both in Rockaway makes me happy . . . makes it all worthwhile. Love, Poppy.*

Lily watched one of the sailors, arms raised, go under the water, and then she didn't watch anymore.

Albert wasn't watching either.

"Don't you like the movie?" she asked.

He shook his head.

"We could leave—" she began, and broke off. She could see the balcony stairs, and the beam from the matron's flashlight bouncing up toward them.

"I was on a ship like that," Albert said.

She blinked. Of course. How else had he gotten here? She had never thought of that. The matron was halfway up the stairs now, looking at them, a frown on her face.

"Albert," Lily began.

"Are you here again?" the matron asked. "I told you last time it's dangerous to climb those steps, and you can't keep coming in here when you don't pay. It was one thing when you were six years old, but . . ."

Lily circled around her, with Albert following, and went down the balcony steps to the first floor. They passed the candy counter and the glass stand with the popcorn piled up to the top, and went out the door.

Behind them was the sound of bombs, and depth charges exploding, and in the marquee's light she could see Albert's face, his blue eyes swimming in tears.

She stood there for a moment, wanting to ask him, wanting to know about the ship, wanting to know what had made him cry. Then she heard the church chimes.

"It's nine o'clock," she said. "Gram is going to have a fit."

They started to run, crossing the street diagonally, just missing an old Chevy with its headlights blackened, its horn blaring at them. They raced past Mrs. Sherman's. "Same cookies," Albert said, breathless, and then around the corner of the As Good As New Shoppe with the dusty hat and coat, the flute and the violin.

By the time they reached the back road Lily had a pain in her chest and a stitch in her side, and Albert wasn't crying anymore. They were both laughing, and he grabbed her hand and pulled her along until they reached her back door.

"Tomorrow," Lily called after him. "See you tomorrow."

"Yes," he said, going down toward the Orbans'.

She went into the house, thinking about tomorrow, thinking about asking him all the things she wanted to know.

Gram was in the kitchen making iced tea, and she poured some for Lily. "I was just getting a little worried," she said.

"I was with Albert," Lily said.

Gram nodded at her. "Good. I'm glad."

Lily went into her bedroom with a glass of lukewarm iced tea and a sprig of mint from Mrs. Colgan's Victory garden. She bent over to run her fingers across her mother's stars pasted in a neat row, still thinking about tomorrow.

Chapter 13

"You can't wear those things," Lily told him after they had fed the cat and were walking along the road. "I'm not going to march along the beach with someone who—"

"You said you wanted to go out on the rocks," Albert said.

"Not with a baby who has beach slippers on his feet," she told him, grinning.

He grinned back, looking down at his feet. "My aunt

said I would come back with cuts from the bar-
nackles . . ."

"*Bar*nacles," she said. "Not bar-*nack*les."

"Same thing." He reached down to pull off Mr. Orban's
slippers and tossed them into the marshes.

She nodded. "Don't worry, they'll still be there
when we get back. Nobody in the world is going to want
them."

She led him down the path, across the sand, toward the
jetty, and began to hop along the rocks. "See," she said,
looking back. "Nothing to it."

He followed her slowly, one foot at a time, wincing.

"Didn't you ever walk around barefoot in Hungary?"
she asked.

"Certainly not," he said. "Do you think we were poor,
that we had no shoes?"

She was laughing again, thinking about her feet, tough
as leather, and Albert, his first summer going barefoot.
She settled herself on the gray triangular rock, way out,
with Albert next to her, the sun on her face, and the
sound of the water lapping against the rocks.

"I want to tell you something," she said after a while. "I
have stars on my bedroom ceiling. My mother pasted
them all up for me when I was a baby. She told my father
she was making a world for me. She said she wanted to
give me the whole world."

Albert wasn't looking at her, his head was turned, but

he was sitting there so still, so unmoving, she knew how hard he was listening.

"I bring one with me to Rockaway every year," she said. "I counted. There are dozens of them left on my ceiling. I'll be thirty or forty before they're all used up."

He nodded a little.

"I never told anyone," she said. "Not even Poppy. I make them presents to me from my mother, every year on my birthday, in July." She took a breath. It was so nice to tell someone about the stars. It was so nice to talk about her mother as if she, Lily, were like everyone else, like everyone who had a mother.

"I know your mother is dead," he said, looking at her now, reaching out for the tiniest second to touch her shoulder. "My aunt told me."

Lily squinted a little, looking out at a curl of smoke from a freighter far out. She waited for him to say something more about them, but when he didn't she began again. "My mother had something wrong with her heart. It was too big. She died right in Poppy's bedroom on a sunny day." She took a breath. "I think that's an all right way to die, but it's not all right that I don't remember her."

"A picture?" he asked. "You have a picture?"

"Poppy has a book with her pictures, but they're blurry, and I don't know what her voice was like. You know?"

She could see his teeth chewing on his lower lip. She

opened the paper bag from Gram: two sandwiches, Spam, apples, Social Tea cookies.

"I hate this," she said, handing one of the sandwiches to him. "Gram does too. After the war we're never going to have one can of Spam again. And Poppy says if we have any left in the kitchen cabinet, he's going to throw them right in the ocean."

Albert had a mouthful of it. "I like this," he said. "I like everything. My grandmother, Nagymamma, loved to cook for me. She said I was her best . . ." He closed his eyes, trying to think.

"Customer," Lily said, watching him nod, as she tried to get her mouth around the word. "Nahj . . ."

"It means big mother, grandmother. The Nagy part just means big."

Lily took a tiny piece of Spam and tossed it into the water. "For the fish," she said. "They probably don't like it either."

"You know my mother is dead too, and my father," he said.

Both, she thought. She couldn't picture what it would be like with Poppy dead. So terrible . . .

"They are dead because they had a newspaper. They wrote bad things about Hitler and the Nazis. And their friends would give out the papers. They were caught one day. The Nazis came to the house . . ."

Lily let out her breath. She didn't want to look in his eyes, but she couldn't help it, she glanced at him quickly, but he didn't look as if he would cry. He was squinting at the water, his eyes dry. "Nagymamma came for me, for Ruth and me, just before they came to our house. And there was no time, not one minute. We did not say goodbye, my mother was running into the kitchen, trying to burn small pieces of paper at the stove, and she looked over her shoulder and told us, '*Szeretlek*,' and then she looked back because the stove was hot and she was almost burning her fingers."

Lily was biting her own lip, chewing on her lip, watching a small fish tear a piece of the Spam, and then another . . .

"It means 'I love you,'" he said before she could ask. "But if they loved us, they would not have done that, they would not have bothered with newspapers. And we do not even know what happened to them. Nagymamma just got a postcard from the police that they were dead."

"Oh, Albert," Lily said, thinking how angry he looked, thinking she was angry too. Poppy should have stayed home.

"And we went to Austria, Ruth and me, in the back of Mr. Kovacs's car, and then across to Switzerland. Mr. Kovacs promised he was going to sneak us all the way across Europe. In Switzerland Ruth was sick with"—he touched his face—"marks."

"Chicken pox?"

He shook his head.

"Measles."

"Yes, and we had been traveling for so long, and Ruth had a fever, a big fever, I knew it. I could not tell anyone." He shook his head, and Lily could see him making fists of his hands.

"We still had to cross the mountains into France," he said. "Mr. Kovacs was pretending we were his children, and the Nazis were there, right there." He was almost breathless, telling her. "We had to get to the ship that would take us to America." He stopped for a moment. "I was afraid they would not let Ruth go."

Lily couldn't look at him. She tore off another piece of Spam for the fish, and the crust of her bread.

"In France she was so thirsty. Her face was red, and she was burning." Albert stood up, balancing himself on the rock, watching the ship, a little closer now. He pointed to the end of the jetty, across the water. "Ruth is in France, and so are the Nazis."

"But how . . ."

Albert sighed. "We were waiting for the ship to take us to America, and this lady who was helping us, this lady with a long gray dress that went to the ground and a cross . . ." He raised his hands to his head. "She was wearing a white . . ." He stopped and frowned.

"Something on her head?" Lily asked. "Was it a nun?"

"Yes. And she said, 'This girl is sick. She belongs in a hospital and not on a ship. She will give the sickness to everyone else.'"

"Measles."

"Yes, but I said it was not measles. I said she could not go to a hospital, but later I fell asleep, and they took her, and I did not even say goodbye."

Lily swallowed.

"Now Ruth is in France until the war is over. The war may last forever, and Ruth is in a convent, with the lady in the gray dress, and the Nazis are right there, and suppose they find out about our newspaper in Hungary?"

"Wait, Albert," Lily began. "Isn't Hungary far away from France? How would they know?"

Albert didn't stop. "Nagymamma said to stay together, no matter what. She said as long as we did, we'd have a family."

He looked around and picked up the bag with the apples.

Chapter 14

*I*t was late on Monday night. Still in shorts and a shirt, Lily lay under her red quilt looking up at the sky. She could see Orion's Belt, and the **W** of Cassiopeia. They were sharp and clear among the other stars in the dark sky. It was a beautiful night, and finally she and Albert were going to watch for convoys.

She thought about it a little uneasily. They hadn't talked about Lily's going to Europe since that day at the beach. Maybe he had forgotten, she told herself, or maybe he had thought it over by now and knew she had been lying.

She turned in the bed, trying to put it out of her mind. Everything was ready for tonight, on the floor. A sweater, two towels, her sneakers tucked in one side of her beach bag, and two bottles of soda jammed into the other side.

If only Gram would go to sleep. Vaguely she heard Gram's radio, the end of *Lux Radio Theatre*, and then music. "Would you like to swing on a star?" She couldn't keep her eyes open.

Then suddenly she was awake, wide awake. It seemed very late, midnight, maybe one o'clock. Gram's radio was off, and all the lights. Lily reached for the screen and pushed it up and out.

She dropped into the rowboat and pushed herself along under the porches. In the light that spilled out from the sides of Mrs. Colgan's blackout shades, she could see a mess of sand crabs hanging on to the pilings.

And at the Orbans', just silence. She sat there as wide awake as if it were the middle of the morning, so angry with herself for sleeping, so disappointed Albert was asleep, she could have cried.

"Too much crying," she said aloud.

"Too much talking to yourself," a voice said, so close she jumped.

Albert dropped into the boat. He was clumsy and splashed water in over the side. "Because of the cat," he said.

She leaned over until she could see the cat's face, its eyes peering out from the front of his open jacket. "Cats hate the water."

"This one does not. I thought you would not come."

She opened her mouth, ready to lie, but raised one shoulder instead. "I fell asleep."

Albert nodded. "It is hard to stay awake sometimes."

Lily pushed the boat out from under the porches. "Here's what we'll do. We'll cut across the bay. That way we can stay away from the surf."

"But it is closer the other way."

"Yes, but it's harder to fight the surf than the bay. If you're going far you want to save your arms."

He nodded, watching her pull on the oars.

"Will you teach me to swim?" he asked after a while.

She blinked. She had been thinking again about Poppy . . . Poppy on a troop ship watching her swim toward him. It was a wonderful dream. "Swim?" she repeated. "Yes. But why can't you swim?"

"I did not have an ocean," he said. Like Margaret in Detroit, she thought.

"I had a river, the Danube." He leaned forward. "It runs between Buda and Pest, but the river is not blue like the waltz. It is gray, and sometimes silver."

Lily didn't say anything. She had never heard of Budapest split up that way in two halves. She'd heard of "The Blue Danube," though. It was one of the songs in her music book for the piano.

It was hard to row now. The marshes were closing in around them, and there was the dry rustle of the reeds hitting the sides of the boat and scraping the bottom.

She could see Playland now in back of them on Ninety-ninth Street, the roller coaster, a dark skeleton, and the Ferris wheel rising up behind it. In front, the boardwalk was misty, the tall lights painted black toward the sea, so German subs couldn't spot ships in the water nearby.

"How long?" Albert asked.

"Long?"

"To learn to swim." He leaned forward. "I want to go with you to Europe."

She opened her mouth. Tell him right now, she told herself. Tell him it's just too far, the water's too rough.

"Lily?"

She sighed. "You could never learn to swim the Atlantic in a summer. It would take months, years to be good enough, fast enough."

"If you can do it . . ."

"I've been swimming since I was four," she said. "And remember that afternoon when I went into the surf after you, I was nearly swept under."

He didn't answer.

She took a breath, trying to think of something to convince him. "You even said you thought I was a better swimmer."

In the dark she could just see him shaking his head. "I

know you are a good swimmer," he said slowly. "I know you were coming for me." He stopped for a moment. "I was . . . I don't know the word . . ."

How could she tell him the truth now? He was the first friend she had ever made. You couldn't count Margaret . . . Margaret, who had been in Rockaway every summer from the time they could walk, from the time they could talk. Albert, a friend, a good friend, Lily's best friend.

" 'Teasing' is the word," he said.

She looked at him. His face was so serious. One hand was in his jacket, petting the sleeping cat. "You do not want to take me," he said. "You think I will not be able to keep up."

"No, it isn't that. Really," she said.

"You think I am a coward because of the plane that day."

She kept shaking her head.

He leaned forward. "It was just that I was thinking it was Europe." His lip trembled a little. "In Budapest, we had a yellow house with birds." He moved his fingers. "They were small birds. Blue ones painted on the house, painted on the window shutters. I had an orange cat too, we called him Paprika, after the pepper. He looks like this cat." He tried to smile. "And my grandmother, Nagymamma, was always telling me to do this and that, like your grandmother."

Lily bit her lip, trying to think of what to say.

"I have only Ruth left. Ruth is my family." He stopped then, and pointed. "Look."

She turned and saw it too. The first ship looked like a flat chunk of coal on the water, so far out she wasn't even sure it was a ship. But then a second one appeared on the horizon, moving out of the mist. It was a huge ship, its top a tangle of turrets and masts.

For a moment, they didn't say anything. They sat there watching, the rowboat rocking gently, until the ship disappeared into the mist again.

"That was a troop ship," she said at last.

Albert leaned back. "Yes," he said, "I know. I will learn to swim, Lily, to keep up, and we will go out there, out to a ship. And then I will go back to Europe to find Ruth."

She began to row again, turning the boat toward the canal, her mouth dry.

Chapter 15

There were two letters the next day, one from Poppy and one from Margaret. Lily managed to pick them up from the mailman before he even hit Cross Bay Boulevard. She'd been waiting on the corner for more than an hour, watching the street as far down as she could see, wondering if Margaret had gotten the letter she had sent. She had told her about Albert and the cat he was calling Paprika.

Lily yawned, tired from last night. Even after she had

tiptoed through the dark kitchen at two or three in the morning and slipped under the red quilt again, she hadn't been able to sleep. She had tossed from one side to the other, thinking about the troop ship, and Poppy, and what she could possibly do about the lie she had told Albert.

Now she took the letters and went straight to Margaret's house, past the bedroom where Paprika slept now, a small orange circle on Eddie's pillow. She climbed the attic stairs and shoved up the window as high as it could go, then took a quick look at the beach. It was still empty at this hour of the morning, litter baskets clean, the sand smooth and even. She had time, plenty of time. She wanted to stretch out this moment with two letters to read. It would be like sucking on a red LifeSaver until it melted into a thin little circle.

She looked at them both, Margaret's as filthy as the first letter she had sent. But this time it was in ink that was blotted and watery as if drops had been spattered on it.

Her father's letter was much neater, much cleaner, and his beautiful clear writing said "Miss Elizabeth Mary Mollahan."

Lily slid her fingernail under the flap and slid out the tissue-paper letter.

"Lily," it began. "My dearest daughter."

She closed her eyes, and held the letter her father had held in his own hands just a few days ago.

She read the rest of it quickly, so fast the words ran

together. He never mentioned that she hadn't said good-bye. He never said that he minded, or didn't mind, only about the war being over, and everything the same again.

I have a picture of you in my head as clear as a photograph to take with me overseas. You're in the boat, and frowning, staring at a skate fish just before you set him free. By the time you read this, Lily Billy, I'll be on my way across the ocean, the faster there, the faster home.

She thought her heart would stop. Her father out there, crossing the Atlantic, part of a convoy, maybe even on the troop ship she and Albert had seen last night.

She couldn't even think about it. She looked at the end of the letter.

Hug the waves for me, and the beach on 101st Street.

And then at the very bottom,

Hug Gram too. She loves you, Lily, more than you know.

Lily wiped her eyes. It was a good thing she had Margaret's letter to think about next, and not having to give Gram a hug.

She looked back at Poppy's letter. At the very bottom he had written:

Don't forget to finish those books, Madeline, *and* A Tale of Two Cities, *and especially* The Three Musketeers.

Lily frowned. Strange that Poppy had written that. He had read *Madeline* to her a hundred years ago, when she was six. How could he have forgotten? And he didn't know she was reading *The Three Musketeers.* She had just taken it from the library on Thursday.

She put her father's letter down carefully near the chimney and opened Margaret's. It started out in the strangest way. No opening, the way Sister Eileen had taught Lily in school. No "Dear Lily." Just

Please go in my living room and get Eddie's picture. Send it right away even if you have to ask your grandmother for the money. Tell her I'll pay her back when the war is over. I can't remember what Eddie looks like and now he's missing in action, isn't it strange, on a beach. It was on D-Day. The telegram didn't come until this morning. He never even got any of the candy.

Margaret

Lily sat there for another minute; then she went down the stairs feeling so dizzy it seemed her feet didn't even touch the steps. She went into the Dillons' living room and reached for Eddie's picture. Her hands were shaking and she knocked it off the table, grabbing it before it hit the floor. Nice catch, Lily, Eddie would say.

Then she was out the door and down the street. She couldn't wait to find Gram, to tell her this awful thing that had happened to Eddie Dillon, to ask for wrapping paper and stamps for the picture.

She went down the road and in the back door, but before she could begin, Gram had started. "Change your clothes, Lily, and get your hat," she said. "Mrs. Colgan told me that Eddie Dillon is missing and—"

"How does she know?" Lily asked.

Gram put her hand up to her mouth. "A phone call all the way from Willow Run to Mrs. Tannenbaum's candy store. We're on our way to church . . . a special Mass, and we're going to pray as hard . . ." She took a breath. "We're all praying, I guess, the whole world, that this will be over soon." She blinked back tears. "And right now, we're going to pray for Eddie, and your father, and Albert's family, and everyone who—" She broke off.

Lily put Eddie's picture on the table next to the couch and went onto the porch to find her Sunday clothes, even though it wasn't Sunday.

Just ten minutes later, she was walking into church, stopping for a quick dip of holy water, and sliding into a pew next to Gram.

As she knelt there and waited for Father Murphy to begin, the sun blasted in around the partly opened stained-glass windows. It felt as if it must be a hundred degrees. The fan in front didn't do any good. It just moved the fringe a little on the banner that hung over their heads.

Father Murphy had hung the banner there himself. On its white background were rows of blue stars, one for each of the men from the parish who were in the service. There was one gold star in the middle. That was for a sailor who used to live near the Cross Bay Theatre. He had been killed at Pearl Harbor. And now, in a day or two, there'd be a silver star for Eddie Dillon, who was missing, lost somewhere on a beach in France, and no one knew if they'd ever find him.

Lily tried to imagine what it must feel like to be Eddie, to have been taken prisoner by the Germans, maybe, or just somewhere by himself, hurt.

It was a desert in that church. She lifted the brim of her straw hat away from her head and fanned the air with her hymnbook, watching Mrs. Orban come up the aisle with Albert, until Gram gave her a poke.

In a moment Father Murphy was out on the altar beginning the Mass, and Lily began to pray for Eddie, and then for Poppy. She prayed for Albert's sister too, and his grandmother.

Next to her, Gram took her silver rosary beads out of their case, and on her other side, Mrs. Colgan opened her missal.

Lily leaned back against the pew, thinking how thirsty she was. She was dying for a glass of orange soda, or maybe a peach with juice dripping. If Mass didn't end soon, and she didn't get something to drink . . .

Gram was looking at her, frowning, so she started to pray again. She prayed for everyone she could think of, even Sister Eileen.

She looked at the stained-glass window. Outside, everything was red or orange or yellow. And inside were the sounds of the fan whirring and feet shuffling. Maybe they'd find Eddie. Maybe he had just gotten mixed up and had to find his way back, or maybe they had made a mistake and some other Eddie was lost.

She sat up straight. She had just thought of something. Eddie's picture. She had left it on the table next to the couch in the living room. How was she going to explain to Gram where she had gotten it? What would Gram say if she knew Lily had been in and out of the Dillons' empty house? Gram would say plenty. Lily'd be in trouble for the rest of the summer. And she'd never get back into Margaret's house until the end of the war.

She tried to figure out what to do. She could feel her heart pounding at the thought of Gram reaching for that picture when they got home. She wondered if Gram had seen her put it down. Gram always saw everything she didn't want her to.

But if she hadn't, if Lily could get to the living room first, she could grab up the picture, and then . . .

And then what? She didn't have a cent since the tan

purse had sunk in the water. How was she going to send it?

And right now, kneelers were banging back and people were standing. Mrs. White was playing the organ, and everyone was singing "Holy God, We Praise Thy Name."

Lily edged herself out of the pew almost before they finished singing. "See you," she whispered to Gram. And before Gram could answer, Lily had ducked ahead of Mrs. Colgan and the other people going down the aisle. She took another quick dip of holy water and raced for home.

Chapter 16

Gram had locked the door, of course. Lily rattled the knob and shoved at it with her shoulder, but it didn't do one bit of good. She was lucky Gram liked to stand and talk to Mrs. Colgan after church for a few minutes.

She went around the back and slipped off her good shoes and socks. She'd have to climb down into the rowboat and shinny up the pilings into her bedroom.

She stopped. A couple of kids from Broad Channel

were rowing out in their boat. They were staring back at her.

She waited a moment, hoping they'd turn away and start fishing or something, but they just sat there, one of them fooling around with the oars, watching her.

Gram would be home in five minutes.

"Forgot my key," she called, and dropped into her rowboat. She wondered what they thought about her wearing a pale yellow Sunday dress as she boosted herself up on the piling and tried to reach the screen.

She couldn't seem to get high enough, and somehow the hem of her dress was soaking wet. Gram would go on and on about how she'd have to wash, starch, and iron it again.

Lily could hear the sound of voices. Gram's voice. Mrs. Colgan's. They were next door, standing there. All they had to do was look down the alley.

She tried to raise her bare foot higher on the rough wood. Any minute she'd have a splinter. And any minute Gram would spot her. She held on to the piling with her legs, and feet, and one arm, as tightly as she could, reaching up for the screen, trying to get her fingernails underneath.

And then, finally, she felt the screen give. She pulled it out, opened it wide, then reached out for the sill, holding on, boosting herself in, just as she heard Gram saying, "Good grief, what's that child doing now?"

She raced through the porch and into the living room, grabbing Eddie's picture, and then raced back again to shove it under her bed. By the time Gram was in the house, Lily was in the bathroom with the door closed and locked, leaning her head under the faucet in the sink, taking deep gulps.

Her dress was a mess, filthy, with a rip in the hem. She took it off as fast as she could, rolled it up in a ball, and reached for her old bathing suit, which was dangling in the shower.

Gram was knocking on the door. "Lily, are you in there? Whatever made you think of getting into the house like that? You could fall and kill yourself. Lily?"

"I'm trying to get my bathing suit on."

"I'd like to see the condition of that dress."

Lily crossed her fingers. "It's all right."

"I'll bet," Gram said.

Lily could hear her footsteps going into the bedroom. She took the dress and slid out the door and onto the porch. She pulled Eddie's picture out from under the bed, wrapped it in a towel, and looked around for a place to hide the wet dress. Under the mattress. She'd figure out what to do with it later.

She was out the door, yelling a quick goodbye before she could hear a word about the piano. But Gram had turned on the news. *"It is estimated that ten thousand have been killed in the invasion of France."*

Lily went up the road to cut across the Orbans' lawn and find Albert.

A moment later, they were rushing down the back road, Albert asking where they were going, why they were in such a hurry.

"To the fishing wharf," she said. "I have to find a purse. A tan one."

"I will help. Where——"

"Under about seven feet of water, and we have to hurry because Gram will be along to capture me any minute."

He shook his head. "Why——"

"She's going to find my soaking wet, ripped Sunday dress. She's going to remember I haven't practiced the . . . You ask a lot of——"

"And what is in that towel?"

"Don't say another word, Albert. Not unless you have a pack of money in your pocket. Otherwise let me think about how I'm going to dive down and find that purse."

"But——"

"That purse has to be somewhere under the water, unless a bunch of pirates have moved in."

"When . . ."

Lily sighed. "Will you stop asking questions? We're in a hurry here."

A truck had scattered gravel all over the approach to the wharf. It was a good thing Albert had shoes on. It was a good thing her own feet were tough.

Not tough enough. By the time they had gotten to the wharf, she was walking on the sides of her feet, hobbling along. "I hope your eyes are good," she said. "I want you to look into this water and tell me . . ."

Albert nodded. She could tell he was trying not to laugh.

"What?" she said.

"You look so . . . so odd walking like that, and your bathing suit . . ."

". . . is a little faded." She looked down. She had put on her oldest one, almost no color left from Gram's Clorox. Too bad. She put the towel with the picture down on a bench and crouched on the edge of the dock to look down into the water. "Dark," she said. "Really dark today, you can't see a thing."

He was looking too. "I see a fish."

"What good is that?" she asked. "It's about two inches from the top. We're looking for a purse on the bottom."

"Down with the bar-nackles," he said, grinning.

She was still smiling as she rolled over the side and hit the water. It was cold this morning, the water rough. She kicked hard to push herself down, opening her eyes in the salt water, trying to see the sand. She swam along the bottom until she thought her lungs would burst, then shot up to the top for a huge gulp of air.

She held on to the wharf for a moment, pushing her

hair out of her face with one hand, and felt Albert grab her wrist. She looked at him through blurry eyes. "What?"

"I have money," he said.

She nodded. "Let me try once more."

But he wouldn't let go. "Let me give you this money," he said slowly, "if it is important. It is important money."

She took another breath. She knew she wouldn't find the purse today. It was so dark below, and it could take hours. She nodded and climbed back up on the wharf.

"It's for Margaret," she told him, going over to unroll the towel, sitting on the bench. She showed him Eddie's picture, with his buck teeth smiling up at them. Then she said the rest in a rush, the words spilling out, trying to make him see what Eddie was like, how much Margaret loved him, how Margaret couldn't remember his face, how she had to send the picture, how . . .

Albert listened; then he touched the edge of the picture. "I cannot remember Ruth's face," he said. "I can remember Nagymamma's. She was sitting in the back of her restaurant the day we went away. She was sewing my coat. The collar was wet when she gave it back to me. It was wet from where she was crying. It crackled when I felt it.

"There is money," he said slowly. "It is in the coat collar. It is Magyar, Hungarian money, and English money, and American money. Nagymamma said when I touched it again to remember . . ." He stopped.

Lily wanted to ask him "Remember what?" but he looked so sad, she just nodded, and used the towel to dry her face.

Chapter 17

GO Molly

"*L*illllyyyy." The voice was loud, sharp.

Her grandmother was standing at the other end of the road, hand shading her eyes.

Caught.

Lily stood there, trying to decide what to do. Then she handed the rolled-up towel with the picture to Albert. "Don't drop it," she whispered.

"Lilllllyyyy," the voice came again.

"What?" She stood there; she didn't move. Gram always wanted her to come when she called, as if she were a cat.

"Lillllyyy."

She gritted her teeth. "Hold on to that with your life, Albert." She started back along the path toward Gram, biting her lip as the gravel jabbed into her feet.

"It's hard to believe you're walking all over the place wearing that bathing suit," Gram said as soon as Lily got close enough to hear. "And where are your shoes? Any minute you're going to get a splinter. Blood poison next. Besides," she rushed on, "you look like a hoyden. I don't know what people will think."

Hoyden. Lily didn't even know what it meant. She sighed, a huge sigh. Let Gram see she thought she was acting like a pain. "I'm going swimming."

"At the fishing dock?"

"Well . . ."

"It's time to practice the piano, Lily."

"I'm not—" Lily began.

"Yes," Gram said. "Your father spent all that money to bring that piano here all the way from St. Albans. For you."

"Poppy doesn't care." Lily shifted from one foot to the other. A stone was digging right through her skin into her bones. Gram was right. She was going to end up with blood poisoning, and Margaret was never going to get Eddie's picture.

"You were the one who wanted piano lessons," Gram said.

Lily could see beads of perspiration on Gram's upper lip. It was hot as a blister, and they were probably going to stand there arguing forever.

Gram was right, though. The piano lessons were all her own idea. But that was last winter. How was she to know that it took forever to learn the piano, that you couldn't even play a decent song like "Mairzy Doats" or "Swinging on a Star" unless you spent your whole life sitting at the piano bench, while everyone else in the whole world was—

"Will you stop daydreaming, Lily?" Gram said. "Get yourself home. Change out of that bathing suit, and practice for a half hour."

Lily didn't wait to hear the rest. Head up, she marched up the road and headed for home.

She threw the bathing suit on the shower floor, put on a pair of shorts and a top, and went to the piano bench. The back door closed a moment later. Gram was home.

Lily looked up at the old alarm clock on top of the piano. One o'clock. She watched the hands for a while. It almost seemed as if they weren't moving. She stood up and put her ear next to it. It was still ticking, but slowly. It would take forever to get to one-thirty.

"Lily?" Gram called from the kitchen.

She curled her fingers over the keys and started in on

the C scale. At the same time, she looked out the window. The sea was tinged with green. Her father would say it had something to do with algae. There was only the slightest swell now, a perfect afternoon to teach Albert to swim.

She closed her eyes, picturing the troop ship they had seen, huge and ghostly in the mist. For a moment she thought about what it would be like if they could do it. Wouldn't it be something if they could get the rowboat close enough to swim the last few feet, the last few yards? Wouldn't it be something if she could teach Albert to swim well enough for that? Even if he could just keep himself afloat, she could help him. And even if it wasn't Poppy's ship, it would be going to Europe. Albert could get to Ruth, and she—

Gram was standing at the living room door. "What are you daydreaming about?" she asked.

Lily frowned. "How much I hate this piano."

"Just try," Gram said. "You can do anything if you really work at it. And you love music."

Lily didn't answer. She started the C scale over and didn't look up until Gram was rattling around in the kitchen again.

You can do anything.

Could she?

What was she thinking of, anyway? What she had to be doing was getting Eddie's picture wrapped and mailed before the post office closed at four. Instead, she was stuck in front of the piano, the keys a little dusty, with the John Thompson book in front of her.

She played the C scale as loudly as she could, up and down, faster, faster. It made a terrific noise. She could hear Gram bang a cabinet door shut. Lily was probably driving her crazy. Terrific. She played around with her hand down low at the bass . . . making up some Hazel Scott boogie music as she went along.

"Lily."

Back to the C scale. The loudest C scale anyone had ever heard.

Nothing from the kitchen.

Lily began to flip through the John Thompson book. Etudes, mazurkas (whatever they were), waltzes. "The Blue Danube."

She picked the music out with one finger. *Da da da da dum dum.* She knew that, she'd heard it before. And that was Albert's river.

She leaned over to reach Gram's atlas in the bookshelf. It was heavy and smelled of the attic in St. Albans. She put it down next to her on the bench and went through the pages, A *Africa, Antilles.* G *Germany.* That was the Nazi place. It showed a little of Hungary on the edge. And there was H *Hungary* two pages later. She tried to spot Budapest, or the Danube River, but all she could find were a bunch of black lines wandering up and down on a yellow blotch that looked like the piece of a puzzle.

In the center of the book was a map of the whole

world. She ran her finger across it . . . from Hungary, to Austria, to Switzerland, to France. She smiled a little. Madeline in the book had been there. She remembered that. Madeline was in Paris.

And so was Ruth.

Lily started in on "The Blue Danube" again with one finger of her right hand, and added some *dum dum*'s with the left hand.

Footsteps were coming around the side of the house. She stood up, still playing, as the top of Albert's head passed the window, then backed up, and his face came into view.

"I thought we were going to . . ." He held up the rolled-up towel.

"Lily, are you playing?" Gram called.

"Hold your horses," Lily told Albert. "I can't get out of here for another twenty-two minutes."

"Lily," Gram called again.

Lily stretched up on the bench to get a good look at Albert. "Besides," she told him, "I've got a surprise for you. Listen to what I'm playing. It's for you, special."

She plunked herself down on the bench again and began to play "The Blue Danube" as nicely as she could.

After a minute, she heard a noise. Was that Albert laughing again? She ended "The Blue Danube" with a crash and began the C scale again.

She could hear Gram at the back door telling Albert to come in for some iced tea while he waited. Good grief.

She opened the John Thompson book to the piece she knew best, the piece she had played a million times last winter. She could hear Gram and Albert talking in the kitchen. The clock wasn't moving.

She began to play. She hit the wrong note with her left pinky. It sounded horrible. For a minute there was silence in the kitchen.

Lily went back to the C scale, played it one last time, but softly now, as if she knew what she was doing. Then she slid off the seat and went into the kitchen. Albert and Gram were talking about music, but not about the piano, about violin music. Albert was telling Gram about the lessons he had taken, and Gram, her head to one side, was listening, nodding.

"Come on, Albert," Lily said, feeling ready to scream, "we've got stuff to do, remember? We can't hang around here all day."

Chapter 18

They were at Margaret's house, sitting on the kitchen floor, with Albert's coat in front of them. The coat was navy blue wool, scratchy against Lily's fingers. She poked Gram's manicure scissors into the collar seam, trying to slide the points under the tiny stitches. Albert was leaning over her shoulder, and Paprika was playing with her sneaker lace.

Lily could feel the perspiration running down her back, the metal scissors sliding in her slippery fingers, when

Albert began to talk, grinning. "Hungarians play 'The Blue Danube' too," he said. "It never sounded like that."

"Like what?"

He looked down at the coat. "Like terrible. Like Ruth plays." He smiled. "Ruth likes to play duets. Loud."

Lily swallowed. "I don't want to play the piano anyway. It takes too much time, and . . ." She'd probably like Ruth. "You should try it," Lily said. "Hanging around on the bench, trying to . . ."

"In my grandmother's restaurant," Albert said slowly, "I played the violin on Sunday. I played that song, and 'Vienna Life,' which is my grandmother's favorite." He stopped. "I loved the violin, Lily. If only I could have taken it with me . . ."

He took a breath. "In Kalocsa's, Nagymamma's restaurant, people ate goulash. They had rolls with sweet butter. For dessert they ate *rigojancsi*, and *gesztenyepüre*, or *palacsintas*."

"What . . ."

"*Palacsintas* are pancakes. They're filled with jam, or chocolate."

Lily looked up.

"Nagymamma gave me plain ones, cold ones, folded over. She put them in my coat pocket when I left."

Lily knew he was ready to cry, but she couldn't think what to say. She just kept snipping at the collar until there was a wide opening in the seam. Without looking up, she pushed the coat toward him and watched as he edged his thumb and index finger gently into the seam. He worked the bills out, laying each one on the floor next to them. "These are Magyar money," he said. "We call them *forints*. And this one is an English pound."

He didn't have to tell her about the next, a fifty-dollar bill, worn and creased. "Nagymamma did not know where we were going. She had to guess about the money."

Lily looked at him, thinking about going to another country without Poppy or Gram, without even knowing where she was going. "Where is . . . ," she began.

Albert reached down for the cat. He held her up to his face, rubbing her soft fur on his cheek. "Nagymamma might be in her house. She might be in prison. I do not know."

Lily thought of her own mother, who had died, but had died of something wrong with her heart, and not in prison, but at home in St. Albans. Lily touched the money on the floor beside her, patted it the way she patted her stars. It was as if she could almost see Albert's grandmother, who had touched it last.

The cat put its tiny needle claws into Albert's shoulder as he reached over to put his fingers into the coat seam again. And now there was a tiny picture with three faces. Albert, of course, with that mop of hair, and an old woman, with a lined face and little round glasses, and a girl. The girl had curls like Albert's, but they were softer, smoother, and she was laughing.

"Ruth," Lily said.

"Yes." Albert looked down at the picture again; then he put it carefully in his pocket. He folded most of the money and put that in his pocket too. Then he handed her the fifty dollars. "Here, for Eddie's picture."

She looked down at the money. "We can't—"

"My grandmother would not mind. She would be glad, I think."

Lily shook her head. "Don't you see? We could never go to the post office with all this money. They'd ask where we'd gotten it. They'd tell my grandmother."

Albert raised one shoulder. "It is too much money, then?"

"More than I've ever seen at once," Lily said.

Albert scooped up the money and stuffed it back into the coat. He sat back on his heels, and put the cat down on the floor. "I guess we should not use the Hungarian money. That is not so much."

Lily grinned. "I don't think so. Nobody around here has ever seen Hungarian money."

"No." He grinned back.

But then Lily heard the church bells. Four times. Four o'clock. The post office was closed, and poor Margaret would have to go another day without the picture.

Lily sighed. "I'll teach you to swim, Albert. We'll go over to the bay now, and I'll figure out how to get money before tomorrow."

"Not the bay," he said, "the ocean."

"Don't be ridiculous."

"I do not know what that means, 'ridiculous.' "

She narrowed her eyes. He knew very well what it meant. "You can't learn to swim in that rough water."

He reached forward to grab her arm. "Do you know that Ruth is waiting for me? Do you know that summer will be over and I will have to go back to Canada . . ."

She nodded. "I'll have to go back to St. Albans, and Sister Benedicta in the sixth grade."

"Please." He was holding her arm so hard now she could feel each one of his fingers tightening around it. His eyes were so blue, and she knew it was never going to happen the way he wanted, and it was all her fault . . . all because of her wild stories.

"Oh yes, Lily. I will learn to swim, and you will row."

She stuck out her lower lip. "If you want to learn, it'll be faster in the bay. And that's my final offer."

"I do not know what that means," he said.

"You don't have to." She unwrapped his hand from her arm and scrambled to her feet. "I'm going to put Eddie's picture back in the living room now, and then I'm going to the bay to swim. If you want to come with me, fine. If not, too bad."

She marched into the living room and dusted the end table with her arm. She thought of Eddie on a beach in Normandy. She'd seen newspaper pictures: Nazi pillboxes set into the rocks, firing; soldiers in the sand, some of them dead, everything confused. They had to get off the beaches before they could begin to free the French cities.

Lily put Eddie's picture on the table and ran her fingers over his face. "Be just a little lost," she whispered. He was smiling in the picture, and she could remember him smiling the same way when she had met him coming out of the movie, or at Mrs. Sherman's, or on the way to church. She wondered if he could count as a friend even though he was much older. "What do you think, Eddie?" she asked.

"Ruth talks to herself all the time," Albert said.

Lily marched past him and out the door. "Are you coming?"

Albert looked up at the ceiling, blinking, trying to decide.

At the same moment, Paprika darted between their legs and out the door.

Albert reached for her, and so did Lily.

She was halfway down the path before they caught up. "She's growing," Lily said, scooping the cat into her arms and bringing her into the house.

Albert nodded. "I could bring her back to Canada, I think."

"Good," Lily said.

"But I am not going back to Canada," Albert said. "Remember? I am going to Europe."

"And I'm going to the bay," Lily said.

"I guess I will come too," he said.

Lily didn't answer. She marched out the door, taking a deep breath.

Chapter 19

Lily had dreamed about Margaret, and Eddie too, but when she awoke, she couldn't remember much more than that. She knew she had been crying in the dream. She was still crying when she opened her eyes.

Gram was standing next to her bed. "It was only a dream, Lily," she said.

Lily leaned up on one arm. Poppy had been in the dream, and Ruth, but Lily hadn't seen her face, just her hair, dark and shiny like Albert's, and there was something about Madeline, the book Madeline.

Gram sat down on the edge of the bed. "What is it? What's the matter?"

"Things are never going to be the same," she said. "Not even when the war is over. Albert might not have his grandmother. He might not have Ruth."

"Everything is so confused over there. A flood of people have come from the rest of Europe, soldiers . . ." Gram sighed. "If our army can get across France, if they can liberate Paris, then maybe someone can get to Ruth." She shook her head. "But you're right, Lily, things won't be the same. We'll all be changed, all of us who lived through this."

"But Poppy said it would be the same."

"I know." Gram patted her shoulder. "He wanted it to be the same for you."

Lily took a breath. She thought of Margaret not remembering Eddie's face. Lily could see his face so clearly, even without the picture.

And Eddie's picture was standing there on the Dillons' living room table. It would take her only five minutes to wrap it and bring it down to the post office this morning. If only . . .

Suppose she told Gram? Gram was sitting there next to her, twisting her long hair with both hands, redoing her bun, looking worried. She could tell Gram she'd never go into the Dillons' house again if she could just get the picture to Margaret.

Gram was standing up now, picking yesterday's clothes up off the floor. "Just a mess in here."

Lily blew breath through her mouth. "I need some money."

Gram blinked. "How did you get from Ruth to needing money?"

"I lost my tan purse," Lily said slowly.

"Oh, Lily." Gram shook her head. "If only you'd think sometimes . . ."

Lily slung her legs out from under her quilt. "Never mind."

"How much?"

Lily twitched one shoulder. "I don't remember."

She went into the bathroom and yanked on her bathing suit. It was still damp from yesterday. Gram was saying something, but Lily turned on the water, blasting it into the sink, and began to brush her teeth.

When she came out, her breakfast was on the table, juice, and Rice Krispies with bananas and strawberries sliced on top, a face with a smiling mouth. And Albert was sitting there, talking to Gram.

Lily ran her fingers through her hair to comb it, then sat across from him. She reached for her juice and took a gulp.

They were talking about music again. Albert was telling Gram that his violin was still in Hungary. "In a blue case," he said, "maybe in my bedroom where I put it." He grinned at Lily. "If I had it here we could play duets."

Gram was laughing, and Lily frowned, but then she laughed too. She could just see skinny Albert playing the violin, playing some wonderful Hungarian thing, and she'd be doing the C scale from one end of the piano to the other.

Gram patted her head. "I love to hear you laugh, Lily."

And Albert nodded. "She is like my sister, Ruth."

Gram was on her way out. "Going to catch a fish," she said. "I'm not going to do another thing all day but spend time in that rowboat and feel that ocean underneath me."

Then she was gone. Lily watched her through the screen, going down to the rowboat, her fishing rod in one hand. And then she noticed Albert was wearing his bathing suit and one of Mr. Orban's old shirts. She knew he was hoping she'd teach him to swim this morning.

Lily stood up, finishing her cereal in a couple of spoonfuls. "I still need the money for Margaret," she said. "I thought of telling Gram . . ."

Albert nodded. "I was thinking about that too," he said. "I have the money."

"No." She shook her head. "Fifty dollars is so much . . . too much."

"From my aunt," Albert said. "I asked her for money."

"Mrs. Orban? You told Mrs. Orban?"

"No. I just asked, 'Could I have . . . ,' and before I could finish she said I should have some money to spend for myself. She said she never thought of it." Albert was pulling money out. A dollar in one pocket. Fifty cents in another.

"I'm so glad." She felt like hugging him. She reached for his hand, warm and dry, and he squeezed back.

They spent the next half hour taking care of the picture. They cut up a paper bag and found cardboard and a ball of string in Mrs. Dillon's closet.

Paprika loved it, the noise and the crinkling of paper as they wrapped the picture in layers of cardboard, and the ball of string to bat across the kitchen floor. But Margaret's house was spoiled for Lily. She wondered what would happen if Mrs. Dillon found out Lily had been in her house all summer. And she would find out. She'd see the picture, and ask Margaret.

Just before they sealed the package, Lily reached for the key on the table, and dropped it inside. "I think we shouldn't come back anymore," she told him.

"All right," he said, thinking about it. "I will take Paprika home with me."

Then they were finished, the package neatly addressed, delivered to the post office, on its way to Margaret at last.

They walked back to the Orbans' with the cat, and by the time Mrs. Orban had made them a picnic snack, Paprika was sound asleep on the couch pillow.

"Now we swim," said Albert. "In the ocean."

"In the bay," Lily answered.

It was hot and humid, and by the time they crossed the

tar road and walked through the sand and rushes toward Jamaica Bay, Lily felt sticky and irritable. She raced into the water, arms stretched, diving deep, feeling the cold bay closing over her, and then she was up again, feeling washed and cool, the sun warm on her face. She brushed her hair back away from her eyes.

Albert. She had forgotten him. He was standing on the edge, his feet dug into the sand, waiting. Lily swam back toward him, as close as she could without scraping the bottom. "You have to float first," she said. "Don't even try to swim yet." She had said that a dozen times the other day.

He took a step into the water. "I have no time to fool around with floating." He had said that a dozen times too. He sounded the way she did over practicing the piano. *I have no time to fool around.*

"Thick as a piece of wood," Sister Eileen would have said about him. It was what she always said when she was teaching math problems and someone couldn't understand.

But there was something else. He was afraid of the water, she was sure of it. She told him to loosen up, to lie back and drift with the water. She told him to unclench his fists and pretend he was one of the reeds, floating.

She told him all the things Gram had told her when she was learning. But it didn't do any good. He couldn't float.

He couldn't swim either. They tried that next. Albert

was like a cat who didn't want to get wet, or a bird weighed down with feathers.

"You are a terrible teacher," he said, trying to joke.

She bit down on her lip, feeling sorry for him. "It takes time. That's what Gram always says." She shook her head. "I can't believe I'm sounding like Gram."

"You are lucky . . . ," he began, and stopped.

She held up her hand. "You don't have to tell me," she said. "I know it. I've been thinking about you and Nagymamma, but you don't know what a pain Gram is."

He smiled a little. "Nagymamma was a pain sometimes too. We had to say *kerem,* and *köszönöm,* and *szívesen* every two minutes . . . 'Please,' and 'Thank you,' and 'You're welcome' . . ."

"She didn't teach you very well," Lily said, smiling too. "Here I'm wasting time showing you how to swim, and you haven't said *kos* whatever once."

"For teaching me how to drown myself?" Then his face was suddenly serious. "It is August, Lily."

She took a breath. "Maybe we should forget about Europe," she said. "Maybe the war will be over in a year."

"A year," he said, sounding as if it were forever.

She tried to think of what else to say, but he was watching her, and she couldn't even look into his eyes. "All right," she said. "I guess we could try again after lunch."

Chapter 20

It was Friday afternoon, lunchtime. The church bells were chiming twelve, Kate Smith was singing "God Bless America" on the radio, and Lily and Gram were having hot tuna fish in tomato sauce. It was horrible, but Gram hadn't caught a fish all week, and Lily hadn't even tried.

"I agree," Gram said. "I can tell by your face you don't like it either."

"I hate this stuff," Lily said, eating as fast as she could. As soon as lunch was over, she and Albert were going to practice again. They'd been in the water so much that Mrs. Orban said they were going to turn into fish. She said it smiling. Even Mrs. Orban could see that Albert was never going to be a fish.

Albert had talked about it last night, said the same thing over and over. "We will row the boat out, stay in it until the ship passes right near us. I will only have to swim the last, smallest bit, and I will be wearing a life jacket . . ."

Lily stared out the window. The water was rough, really rough. Even though the sun was shining, the water had a dark look to it, and she could see whitecaps at the end of the canal. They couldn't swim this afternoon. Alleluia. What instead? The movies? Fishing. Yes, fishing. They hadn't done that once this summer.

Gram was saying something, had been talking for minutes. Something about forgetting. Lily looked up.

"You asked me for money," Gram said.

Lily took another mouthful, trying not to taste the fish. "I don't need it anymore."

"I'm sorry," Gram was saying. "I asked you how much you wanted, but you were getting dressed, and . . ." She raised one shoulder. "I never thought about it again until just this minute."

Lily looked up, trying to remember. How much? Gram had said. How much had she lost? How much did she need? Lily felt a quick flash of guilt.

Gram looked hot and tired. It was boiling in the little kitchen. Even with the shades halfway down, the sun lay in patches on the table, the counters, and the floor. Suppose something happened to Gram someday?

"Never mind," Gram said. "I'm going to make up for it . . . and for the tuna too. I have a letter, two letters for you. One from Poppy, and one from Margaret." She sighed. "Poor Margaret."

Lily put her fork down. That's what she got for spending the morning swimming. She had missed the mailman. Now Gram would be reading over her shoulder.

Gram slid the letters over to her. Margaret's filthy as always, Poppy's, airmail, tissue-paper thin. "The mailman was looking for you," Gram said.

Lily didn't answer. She opened Margaret's first, a long letter in pencil, hard to read in Margaret's scrawl.

Thank your grandmother for the letter.

Lily looked up quickly. Gram wasn't leaning over her shoulder after all. She was turning the pages of her newspaper, *The Wave*. Lily looked down again, finding her place.

Thank her for the picture of Eddie swimming and those funny stories about when he was little. She made me laugh. I felt so bad. She misses your father. She calls him Jerry isn't that

*strange I always think about him as Mr Mollahan. We still
don't know anything about Eddie.*

*Love Margaret.
How's the house?*

"You wrote to Margaret? You sent a picture?" Lily
asked. "You didn't tell me that."

Gram pushed a strand of hair off her forehead. "I knew
how she felt. Suppose it was Poppy?"

Lily sat looking at Gram from the corner of her eye.
She'd never thought about Gram missing Poppy, not once
in all these weeks. She pushed Margaret's letter across the
table to her, then took a breath. She had forgotten the
house part. But Gram didn't seem to notice anything
strange about Margaret's mentioning her house.

Lily reached for Poppy's letter, the best for last. It was a
funny letter, Poppy reminding her of the time they
painted the window and the screen had fallen over the
edge of the porch and floated away. *Your fault*, Poppy had
written for fun. They both knew it had been his fault.
And then in the end, there was more about books. *Don't
forget to read* The Story of Roland *again, and* The Promise.
*Go to the library for them. See Mrs. Hailey. She knows every
book in the world!*

Lily had read *The Story of Roland* with Poppy last winter, but not the other. She and Albert could take a quick
trip to the library after they went swimming. Why not?

136

Gram had finished Margaret's note and was looking out the window now. Her gray eyes were sad.

"Here," Lily said, feeling generous. "Read my letter from Poppy. It will make you laugh."

Lily took the last bite of tuna, thinking about a night last summer when they had eaten the same thing. It was almost dark, after Poppy had come. They had been talking, laughing. It was something about Gram's fishing being so bad they had to eat canned tuna. And outside, the fireflies had floated over the porch.

"Do you remember . . . ," Gram began as she put the letter down.

"Last summer?" Lily asked.

"No, the year of the hurricane," Gram said.

Lily thought about it, the bay water, usually flat, crashing up against the pilings. Boats, let loose, filled with water, breaking apart and sinking. Their own rowboat, upside down, looking like a walnut shell, under a couple of feet of water.

"What made you think of that?" she asked.

"I have a memory of your father, coming down the road, his shoes off . . ." Gram bit at her lip. "His suit pants were rolled up to his knees, full of mud, his newspaper—"

"—soaking wet, covering his head," Lily said.

"And we laughed," Gram said.

Lily nodded. She remembered how funny her father had looked, hopping along. She and Gram had watched from the kitchen door, so happy he was home.

And now Gram was crying. Lily couldn't believe it. She had never seen Gram cry. Lily's mouth was suddenly dry. "Why . . ."

Gram shook her head, her mouth trembling, trying to smile. "I guess I miss your father."

Lily stood up, about to go to her, to put her arms around her.

"By the time he comes home," Gram said, "you'll be playing the piano for him."

Lily veered off to the sink. She slid in her dish with a couple of other dishes and ran water over them. She could see Gram standing to put a bottle of milk into the refrigerator. No one would ever know tears had been in her eyes a moment ago.

Lily wiped her hands on a towel. "We're going to swim, Albert and me. And then go to the library."

Gram nodded, and Lily was out the door, around the side porch, and down into the rowboat. Albert was sitting there, waiting for her, looking even skinnier than usual with the huge orange life jacket around him.

She hopped into the boat and began to row past the houses, angling toward the marshes, leaning forward to keep the sun out of her eyes.

"I hope I can do this." Albert sounded worried.

Lily rowed across the bay, moving swiftly, pulling hard on the oars. She wouldn't have to tell him after all. He'd tell her to go without him, and then she'd say . . .

She looked across at him. His face was white, his lips pale. She threw the anchor into the water. "Now we'll go over the side. The boat isn't going anywhere, and if you really get in trouble you can reach for one of the tall reeds."

Albert's eyes were almost closed.

"I'll go first," she said, and went over the side slowly, carefully, so the boat wouldn't rock. She hung on to the edge with both hands for a second, getting used to the feel of the water, cool on her body, then slipped away from the boat. "Don't forget, Albert. Keep your mouth closed. Last time . . ."

"I know." He was clumsy getting over the side, rocking the boat enough to create small waves. And then he was in the water, reaching up to grip the side.

"Let go," she said. "You've got on a life preserver. You can't sink." She grinned. "Even you can't sink."

He shut his eyes and let go.

"Good," she said, treading water. "Feel how lovely. Not too cold. Open your eyes, will you?"

He struck out with one arm and then the other.

"Kick your feet, remember?"

He opened his eyes. "Too much to remember all at once." He was out of breath.

"Take your time."

He started again, head high.

"Not bad, not bad at all, but wait a minute." She swam

over to him, thinking he looked like a turtle. A land turtle. "What do you think will happen if you just put your head in the water?"

"Remember last time?"

"Yes, but your mouth was wide open. Duck your head. Just feel . . ."

He took a deep breath and leaned forward. A moment later he was up again. "I can hardly stay down." He sounded surprised, pleased.

"See," she said. "Nothing's going to happen."

He nodded once, and then a second time. "You are right, Lily."

He leaned into the water again, raising his arm. She could see his feet behind him, kicking a little, kicking harder. He was moving. He was swimming.

She watched as he circled the boat, then floated, his hands pale in the water, fingers spread. "I am swimming," he told her.

"I know," she answered him, thinking she had done it. She had taught him to swim. And then something else. She'd have to tell him they couldn't go to Europe.

Chapter 21

The sea was high today. Lily tried to remember when she had last seen it this way, yellow-green water reflecting the strange color in the sky. They had rowed only a short way from the porch, still in the bay, to fish.

She dropped her fishing line over the side of the rowboat. The day was hot, the wormy bait sticky on her fingers. She felt sick with the smell of it, sick thinking about what Albert would say when she told him.

It had been a terrible day from start to finish. The

library had been closed for days, and when they had finally gotten there this morning, Mrs. Hailey hadn't been one bit friendly. "Bringing sand in on your feet," she had grumbled. "Leaving a trail behind you like Hansel and Gretel."

And then when Lily had tried to get both books, The Story of Roland and The Promise, Mrs. Hailey had looked up over her glasses. "Don't you have a book at home, overdue?"

Lily had remembered she had left The Three Musketeers at the beach, and when she began to make something up, Mrs. Hailey had sighed. "Don't, Lily," she had said.

It had ended up that all she got was The Story of Roland, which she had already read, and what good was that? And she had thought Mrs. Hailey was her friend.

Albert was going on about meeting a ship. "It will go to France. I think it will. I know it will. I will start at Paris. I will go to every hospital. I will go everywhere. I have money. I will buy what I need. I will find her, do not worry."

Werry.

Lily took a breath. "Who's going to take care of Paprika?"

Albert looked over the side of the boat, almost as if he could see the bottom, almost as if he were searching for a flounder. "The Orbans, of course. They will do that for me. Don't you think so?"

"I have to tell you . . . ," Lily began.

But Albert was singing now. He paused. "I will teach her this song from your radio," and he began again. " 'You've got to ac-cent-tchu-ate . . .' "

"Albert."

" '. . . the pos-i-tive.' " He shook his head. "Did you ever notice, American songs are strange. I do not know what they mean most of the time."

"You're scaring the fish with that noise."

"Not my fish." He raised his line. "On the ship last time I was always thirsty, and the water tasted warm. We have to bring juice." He nodded. "Yes. And maybe fruit. Nagymamma always said fruit was important. In the winter we ate tangerines."

"And how would you carry all this?"

"In my pocket."

"Very interesting," she said, forgetting for a moment what she had to tell him. "You have pockets in your bathing suit?"

He waved his hand. "I did not think of that."

"Albert . . ."

"No matter. I will drink warm water, and go without fruit if I have to."

"Albert . . ."

He looked across at her.

She took a breath. "We can't go."

He turned his head, watching her, and she knew he was seeing the tears in her eyes. She opened her mouth to say she had changed her mind, that she'd heard that the convoys were moving out to sea farther south, but lying to Albert wasn't like lying to anyone else. He had a way of looking at her as if everything she said was important, serious or funny, interesting to him somehow. How could she tell him something she had just made up? How could she lie again?

"I lied," she said.

She could see the beginning of a quiver on his line. He was about to catch something . . . something small, maybe a sea robin. But he didn't take his eyes off her, and her mouth was so dry she could hardly speak.

"What do you mean you lied?" he asked. "You mean you do not want to go with me? You are still worrying I am a coward because of the plane, because it took me so long to swim?"

"You're not a coward, Albert."

He frowned. "I am not afraid of anything."

"I tell lies," she said, almost whispering. "I tell people that my aunt is a spy. I say my father is in the Secret Service. I tell you I'm going to take a ship when I know the ships are too far out, that they seem closer than they are, and the sea is too strong and rough."

"But I can go," he said. "I am not afraid."

She felt tears running down her cheeks and reached up to wipe them away.

"You are crying because of your father?" he asked.

She nodded. "And because of you. You thought I would help you go back . . ." She took a breath. "I said it because I didn't say goodbye to my father," she said. "I sneaked out of the house, and I never went back to say goodbye, and now . . ."

Albert reached out. He held his hand over her wrist just the way Poppy had. "Lily," he said. "I lie too."

She shook her head. "Not the way I do, every minute."

"Yes, because I am afraid." For the first time he saw that the line was wiggling, that he surely had a fish. "I will pull this fish up and set it free," he said. "Then I will tell you the truth. And you will know why I have to go on this ship back to Ruth."

Chapter 22

*L*ily walked down Cross Bay Boulevard. She'd been looking for the mailman all afternoon. Just then he rounded the corner. "I've been waiting forever," she told him.

"It's too hot to walk fast," he said. "But I have something for you." He pulled out a letter.

"Poppy," she said. She took it from him, smiling. She didn't wait to open it. She leaned against the window of the As Good As New Shoppe to tear open the thin white envelope. Mr. Rowley, the owner, was moving things around. No more straw hat, and the violin was gone. Instead, he was dragging a huge moose head to the windowsill. It must be a thousand years old, Lily thought, and it will be in the window for another thousand.

She looked down at Poppy's letter, ran her fingers over the handwriting she loved. He didn't say much about himself, but about the end of the summer, and Lily's going back to St. Albans. He asked about how many books she had written.

She looked at the moose head. "I've written about as much as you have," she said under her breath. But never mind, there'd be plenty of time for that when school began.

She turned the page over. There was more about books. Poppy wrote about *Madeline* again, and *A Tale of Two Cities*. "And remember *The Promise*," he had written. "That's the key to it all."

There was always something, Lily thought, as she headed for home. Before she went to the library, she'd have to find the *Three Musketeers* book.

It wasn't easy. Bent almost double, she searched under the boardwalk for an hour. Up above, she could hear thunder, and once in a while she could see streaks of heat lightning in the distance.

But at last she spotted the book. It was propped up

against one of the posts, a little wrinkled, a little sandy, but she blew on the pages, and went off to the library to ask the world's crabbiest librarian to find *The Promise* for her.

Mrs. Hailey looked up as Lily laid the book on the desk in front of her. "Ah, Lily," she said smiling. "I've been looking for you. I know I was crabby the other day . . ."

Lily began to shake her head, began to say no, but then just smiled and rolled her eyes.

They both laughed.

"I was hot and tired, and I didn't need one more story about a lost book," Mrs. Hailey said.

"That's all right," Lily agreed. "I found the book anyway."

"Another reason I'm glad you're here," Mrs. Hailey said. "I searched and searched. I even called the library in Jamaica. Your father really knows books, but this time he's wrong. There's no children's book called *The Promise*."

"I'll tell him," Lily said. She thought for a moment. "How about *A Tale of Two Cities*?"

"Lovely book. A little hard, but worth it." Mrs. Hailey plucked it off the shelf in back of her and stamped it with the end of her pencil.

Outside the window was a sudden flash of lightning, and then a clap of thunder, so close they could feel the vibration.

Mrs. Hailey shivered. "I'm glad it's closing time. And you should be home too."

Lily waved her hand. "No rush. Gram is sewing with her club. She left supper for me in the refrigerator."

Mrs. Hailey glanced out the window again. "We're going to have a storm."

Lily nodded. "I'm on my way anyway." She tucked the book under her arm and was out the door and down the street, feeling the wind pushing her along.

By the time she crossed to the other side of Cross Bay, it had begun to rain. The wind picked up papers and swirled them into doorways, and huge drops spattered the dust along the boulevard.

Lily began to run, thinking about Albert. She had told a hundred lies, a thousand lies, but Albert had told only one. And it wasn't really a lie. All he had done was keep his eyes closed.

She sighed.

He had sat in the boat the other afternoon and closed his eyes to show her. "I was afraid of the Nazis in France," he said. "Very afraid."

Lily had backstroked the oars gently, keeping the boat away from the porches, as he told her the rest.

"The lady with the gray dress came with the people from the hospital," he said, "and I closed my eyes. It wasn't that they were mean. Ruth was sleeping, and one of them said, 'Poor little girl.' They took her in an ambulance. I knew if I opened my eyes they would take me with them. I could have stayed."

"It's all right." Lily could see his hands clasped tight

together, and his knees clenched. He was shaking as if he were cold on that hot afternoon. "I would have been afraid too," she said. "I would have shut my eyes."

"I wanted to come to America," he told her. "I wanted to be safe. I didn't even say goodbye."

"Oh, Albert," she had said, knowing how he felt.

"I left Ruth . . . ," he had begun again, so quietly she had to lean forward to hear him, ". . . and Nagymamma said to stay together, to be a family."

Lily had begun to talk. She said everything she could think of, everything she thought Gram might have said. "The war will be over," she told him, "and Ruth will come, and maybe even Nagymamma. We'll all be in Rockaway together."

"Nagymamma was very old. I think maybe . . ." He stopped. "Ruth has no family except me. She has no one special to watch out for her."

Lily could see him looking toward the sea, the waves high, breakers crashing onto the beach. He shivered.

"The lady leaned over. I felt her putting something into my coat pocket. It's Ruth's address. I will show you someday." He shook his head. "What good is it? I cannot write to her. I have to go back and get her somehow."

"You can't go back," Lily said. "You can see the water. It would never work. It's my fault. I shouldn't have . . ." She bit her lip. "It was my lie."

"I want to tell you something, Lily," he said. "I was so

angry, so sad when I left Hungary. I told Nagymamma I would be angry and sad forever."

Lily looked up. It was hard to see his face because her own tears were blinding her.

"Do you know what Nagymamma said?" he asked. "She said I would be happy someday. She said I'd have a friend, a good friend. It's almost as if she knew about you."

"We'll make a pact," she said.

"What is that?"

"We won't lie. We'll be brave."

"Yes," he said.

"But not so brave to try for the ship. Promise?"

Now, in the pouring rain, Lily was reminded of her father. She reached the house and pulled open the kitchen door, thinking she was going to write and ask him about the book *The Promise*.

There was another tremendous streak of lightning. It lit up the porch, and the whole of the sky, and she could see in the distance a rowboat at the edge of the bay, about to cross through the edge of the marshes.

It was Albert.

Chapter 23

*L*ily couldn't see light in any of the houses along the row, not even glimpses from the edges of the blackout curtains. Everyone was gone, it seemed. Gram wouldn't be home for an hour, and the Orbans were probably shopping, caught somewhere in the rain.

A moment later, she slid down the ramp into the rowboat and began to row toward the marshes. Another bolt of lightning lit the bay, and beneath the seat in the stern she could see something almost hidden against the anchor. It was Paprika, small and wet, shivering, terrified.

There was no time to take her back, no time to dry her off. She'd have to stay there huddled under the seat until later, until Lily persuaded Albert to come back.

He hadn't promised he wouldn't try it, but she thought she had convinced him. How could he have thought he could do it alone, she thought, in a storm like this?

The bay was rough with whitecaps, and the rain, pelting the water, slanted toward her, pushed by the wind. She was soaked through, her hair hanging in strings, dye from her shorts running blue over her legs.

A puddle of water was gathering in the bottom of the boat. She knew she should scoop it out with the old coffee can they kept for bailing, but there wasn't time for that either. She kept her eyes focused on the marshes so the lightning would show her how far Albert had gone.

She was lucky he was a poor rower . . . unlucky that in the center of the bay the waves were beginning to rise so high that the boat dropped steeply at times, and the oars didn't hit the water with every stroke.

She couldn't stop thinking of Poppy telling her that someday the war would be over and everything would be the same. She couldn't imagine it. And she didn't even know where Poppy was.

That last night in the boat he had promised her he'd let her know.

Promised.

Something tugged at her mind, and then it was gone.

She was across the bay past the marshes she couldn't see, and across the channel. The pull of the sea was much stronger now, and as she looked back, she couldn't see the entrance to the bay anymore, even though she was just a few strokes away. For a moment she could see the misty beams of the tall lights on the boardwalk; then they were hidden again as the rowboat slid into the trough of a wave.

Then, above the sound of the rain and the waves, Lily heard another sound, the sound of a motor. A small boat, she thought, a fishing boat, or maybe a cutter, and nearby. The sound was comforting. She didn't feel so alone, even though she couldn't see it.

And just ahead of her was Albert. He had heard the sound too. In the next lightning flash, she could see him turn, looking over his shoulder.

"Wait," she called. "It's not a ship, not a troop ship. Don't, Albert . . ."

He couldn't hear her, but in another flash he saw her, she was sure. And the rest of it seemed to be in slow motion. The next wave was so swollen, so tremendously high, that it pulled his boat up, and up, and the boat poised there on the crest for an instant, motionless. She could see him clearly, the orange of his life jacket standing out even in the darkness.

Then, as the wave slid out from under the boat, she

could see the forward part rising, almost straight up. Lily watched it, breathless, as it slid back, and in that second, Albert was tossed into the sea.

She could see the orange life jacket a little longer, but after only seconds a wave pulled her boat in one direction and Albert in another and he disappeared.

She kept calling, kept trying to turn the boat in circles, glancing at the lights on the boardwalk to mark her place, watching for the streaks of lightning to show her where he was.

She veered away from his empty boat, which was spinning first high on a wave, then into the crest. In another flash she saw him again, just the quickest glimpse, the orange life jacket, and his dark head above the water.

"I'm here," she yelled, not sure he had heard her, or even seen her, and then another wave came, a mountain of a swell that moved toward them, pushing Albert toward her. Lily could see him turning toward her, his mouth open. He was gulping water, and she reached out, and by some miracle, her hand hooked around the top of the jacket. She held it, feeling her nails rip, but knowing she wouldn't let go, even if she was pulled out of the boat.

But the wave was past them now, and the water grew calm just for the second he needed to grip the boat, and she pulled at his jacket with both hands until he tumbled into the boat.

He lay there in the bottom, the water washing over him, taking deep breaths. *"You promised,"* she wanted to say, even though she knew he hadn't. But she knew it was her fault, all her fault because of her lies, and she told herself she'd never tell another lie if she could just get him back safely.

And now Albert was up on the seat, briefly raising one shoulder in the air, coughing, and reaching out to touch her hand. Lily turned the boat back into the bay, rowing toward the houses, watching him trembling with the cold. Finally she nosed the boat in under the porch, the lights on above, and Gram waiting, and watched as Paprika, a furious ball of orange fur, streaked out of the boat and up the path away from them.

Chapter 24

They went into the kitchen, the three of them, Gram sliding the teakettle onto the stove as soon as they were in the door. "Change your clothes, Lily," she said, "and find something of your father's that Albert can wear."

And twenty minutes later, they were huddled around the table, hair damp, but wearing dry clothes, with Gram's knitted afghans around their shoulders.

"It was my fault," Lily said slowly. "I told him we could get a ship to Europe. And he was trying . . ."

"Oh, Lily," Gram said.

Albert's eyes were on her. "I never really thought we could go. It was a dream. A dream like thinking someone will find Ruth . . ." He sighed. "I just wanted to see the ships one more time. I wanted to think about the ships going to Ruth."

Lily nodded, thinking that she had dreamed the same thing, going to Poppy, finding Poppy.

"When I started, it was not even raining. I just row so slowly . . . ," he said. "I would not have gone without you." He shook his head. "And now I have lost the boat."

"And we might have lost you both." Gram scraped back her chair. "Don't you know that this is what it's all about? Nagymamma sending you and Ruth away from her so you'd be safe? And your parents publishing a newspaper, helping to win the war, so you'd have a good life?"

"For me? My mother and father?" Albert was nodding. "I have never thought about that. I have just never thought . . ."

Gram turned to Lily. "And Poppy, who could have stayed right here . . . He went for you, Lily, and I had to let him go. My son." She turned her head a little. "It was so hard."

Gram didn't say anything else for a moment. She looked like herself, stern, frowning a little. But then she put her hand on Lily's cheek. "But worth it. Worth the price to keep you safe."

Before Lily could say anything, Gram pushed back the

flowered curtains and went into her bedroom. "I have something for you, Albert." She came back carrying a blue case.

"From the window," Lily said, realizing. "From the As Good As New Shoppe."

Gram smiled. "I'll have to swap fish every week for this violin for the next two summers."

And Albert was reaching for the violin, running his hands over the case, then snapping it open to look at the shiny wood and pluck the strings.

"I know about Nagymamma," Gram said. "I know she'd want this for you."

But by this time the violin was under Albert's chin. For a moment he tightened the strings, his head turned to one side. Then the kitchen was filled with the sound of a Hungarian song, fast, and sharp, and beautiful.

And Gram was nodding. "See, Lily," she said, "if you'd only practice . . ."

And at that moment, Lily remembered Poppy's letter. *Give Gram a hug. She loves you more than you know.*

She sat back, glad Gram was there in the kitchen instead of far away like Nagymamma. She listened to Albert playing, his head bent over the violin, his fingers moving on the strings, as the sound of the rain grew less and then stopped altogether, and in the window she could see a pale, late sun edge the horizon.

"This one, this waltz," Albert said, "is Nagymamma's favorite."

But before he had played more than two or three notes, Lily remembered something else. "Good grief," she said, "my library book."

"The book in the rowboat?" Albert asked. "It must be soaking wet."

"Come on, Albert," she said. "We have to get it out of there, dry it off, something. And we have to look for Paprika."

They left Gram with her tea, and as Lily went out the door, she turned back to see Albert leaning over Gram at the table, kissing her cheek. *"Szeretlek,"* he said.

Then Lily was down in the boat, with four inches of water in the bottom, handing it up to him. "Mrs. Hailey will have a fit," she said. "She said it was a lovely book."

Albert looked at it, water dripping from the edges, the dye running. "I know this book," he said. "I have read it in school. It's about the French Revolution, a million years ago."

Lily raised her hand. "Albert," she said. She sank down on the wet seat, her feet sloshing in the water. "Oh, Albert. The French Revolution. I know where my father is."

She looked up. "He's been trying to tell me all these weeks. *Madeline* and *The Three Musketeers. Roland,* the French hero. All in France. That's why he sent me to Mrs. Hailey. He knew she'd tell me there wasn't a book called *The Promise."*

Albert was frowning. He didn't know what she was talking about.

"His promise, Albert. That's what he meant. He promised I'd know where he was, that he'd tell me without the censors knowing. It took me all this time."

And she began to smile, because Albert looked so silly standing on the dock with Gram's pink afghan over his shoulders and the dripping book in one hand, and because she knew where Poppy was. And then she remembered the war news, and all the men who were being killed as the army tried to fight its way across France. Let Poppy be all right, she thought.

Chapter 25

L ily counted the days on her fingers. It was almost time for St. Albans, almost time for the sixth grade and Sister Benedicta.

It was almost time to say goodbye to Albert.

They had sent the letter to Poppy two weeks ago, she and Albert, both of them writing together, trying not to blot the tissue-thin paper. Albert had showed her the creased scrap of cardboard with spidery black writing before he copied it carefully: *Ruth Orban, Maison-Mère Filles de la Sagesse, Rue de la Santé, Paris.*

"We can't count on it," Lily had told him. "Maybe I'm wrong, maybe Poppy's not in France."

"Yes," he said. "I know."

She didn't mean it, though. She knew Poppy was there. She was sure of it. And she kept remembering what he had said in the rowboat. *"Right behind the armies will be people like me. We're the ones who'll help put Europe back together again."*

Find Ruth . . .

For the first time, Lily paid attention to the war. Mrs. Hailey lent them a huge map of France. They hung it in Gram's kitchen, and tried to guess how long it would take the Allies to get from Cherbourg, to Caen, to Rouen, and at last to Paris. And as Lily moved her finger slowly from one city to another, she could almost feel Poppy there.

In the meantime they swam and fished. Albert caught a skate and a sea robin and put them gently back into the water. Lily caught a fluke once and, for the first time, a flounder.

And then on Tuesday they had an argument. They didn't speak to each other for three days, and all because of the new movie at the Cross Bay Theatre.

"I am not climbing those stairs," Albert had said. "I am paying money, and I am walking in through the front door. I am not a thief."

"I don't have money," Lily had said.

"I will lend—"

"No."

"I will give—"

"No." She didn't know why she was so stubborn, why she was so angry with him. She spent two afternoons in the rowboat by herself before he appeared again at the dock.

"I have come to swim," he said at last.

"So swim," she said. "You don't need me." But she was pulling the rowboat in, ready to put on her bathing suit and go with him.

"I'm not a thief either," she told him.

He raised his eyebrows.

They started along Cross Bay Boulevard, waving to Mrs. Sherman, who was sweeping her walk across the street.

"Well, all right." Lily spoke as if Albert had said something. "I'll pay. I'll save my money this winter, and next summer . . ." She bit her lip and glanced at him. She knew he'd be thinking the same thing. Would he come back next summer? Would he ever come back?

"I know why you were angry," he said. "When people go away . . ."

She nodded. "Yes."

They had just passed the As Good As New Shoppe when the door banged open in back of them. "Mrs. Sherman," called Mr. Rowley. "The radio. Turn it on. The news. Paris is free."

Across the street Mrs. Sherman flung out her arms. "Free." Her face was turned up to the sky. "That beautiful city."

"They're going to keep going now," said Mr. Rowley, "those soldiers of ours, right to Germany."

Lily stopped walking. Next to her Albert had stopped too. "Free," she whispered.

The mailman rounded the corner. "Have you heard the news?" he called. "It's the beginning of the end. Next summer we'll have lights on the boardwalk, and the guys will be home."

Lily grabbed Albert's arm. "You'll be able to write to Ruth. The Nazis will be gone and . . . Poppy will go to her."

"Ruth," Albert was saying at the same time. "Ruth is there. I wonder what she is doing now, at this moment."

Two days later, they could guess. Albert treated Lily to the movies and to a bag of popcorn, and they watched *The Eyes and Ears of the World* four times.

They saw pictures of the great Cathedral of Notre-Dame and heard the story of the little plane that had flown just above its dome on Thursday. It had dropped the message: "Tomorrow we come."

Next to her, Lily could see Albert clutching the arms of the chair. His face was turned away from her, and she knew he was crying.

She cried too, but they weren't the only ones. She could hear the sounds of crying all through the theater. They watched the main street of Paris, the Champs Elysées, filled with two million people, old women with white hair, men with flags, children, and nuns. Young women were throwing kisses at the American soldiers, who were riding on tanks covered with flowers.

In one huge voice, the French were shouting, "*Merci. Merci. Merci . . .*"

Albert whispered it, "*Köszönöm.*"

And Lily too, "Thank you."

Then the tricolor, France's flag, went up on the cathedral, and people began to sing the French anthem, the "Marseillaise."

Lily and Albert leaned forward, staring at the faces surrounding the cathedral, looking for Ruth, looking for Poppy. Lily could almost picture them there, together.

At last they stood up, blinking, and went through the lobby. "Of course, we could not see them," Albert said. "So many people."

"Of course not," Lily said. "But we know they were there. And someday we'll ask . . ."

Albert was smiling at her, nodding. "And they will tell us."

They headed back toward Lily's. By this time it was almost dark. They'd been in the movie for hours. Overhead the first star was just visible.

She looked up at the sky. Only a few days were left of

summer. And then she thought of the stars on the porch wall in back of her bed. Her mother's stars. She'd peel one off for him. He could paste it on the little cardboard with Ruth's address. Yes, she thought, she'd give it to him before they left.

Chapter 26

St. Albans, 1945

*L*ily was going to be late for school. She pulled on her uniform and ran a comb through her hair. Downstairs Gram was calling, "Don't forget a sweater, and if you're looking for your boots . . ."

Lily sighed. Next Gram would remind her she had left them on the living room rug again. Lily took a quick look out at the white flakes that had begun to drift down. It had been a long winter. She was tired of snow and sleet, sick of chapped lips and colds, and the wind that rattled against the windows. It seemed as if summer would never come, and worse, that the war would go on forever.

She looked around for her books and her journal, ELIZABETH MOLLAHAN, MY THOUGHTS.

She had written her way through the winter . . . to Poppy, and Albert, and Margaret, but most of all in the journal, to Sister Benedicta. Once she had told about the way the sea rolled and churned when it stormed, and how homesick she was for Gram's house on stilts. Another time she had written about Albert, and the day they had said goodbye.

Lily closed her eyes now, thinking about that last afternoon of the summer. The tide had been high and the ocean a deep blue. She had walked with him out to the jetty. They had stood there balancing themselves on the gray rock, and she had taken the star out of her pocket for him then, one of her mother's from the porch wall. Almost without thinking, she had stood on tiptoes to give him a quick kiss on the cheek, and they had both laughed.

Lily thought about Sister Benedicta now. "Some people never have a friend like that," Sister had said. "You were both lucky, Lily, even if it was only for the summer." And then she had tapped one finger on the journal. "You have promise, Lily."

"How did you know about that?" Lily had asked, thinking about Poppy and the books.

But Sister hadn't meant that at all. "I mean promise as a writer," she had said.

Lily started downstairs for breakfast this morning, saying the word in her head, *promise*, half listening as Gram called, "Hot cereal on a cold day."

Lily hated hot cereal. "I'm late," she began. "I don't have time for . . ." But she never finished the sentence. She heard the noise of the key in the front lock, and stopped halfway down the stairs. She had heard the sound of that key so many times, and now she felt the blast of cold air coming up as the door opened. She felt as if she couldn't breathe because she knew who it was, knew who it had to be.

And then she was flying down the stairs, reaching out, as Poppy pushed a duffel bag in ahead of him, and held out his arms for her. A moment later, Gram came down the hall. He held them both, the three of them rocking for a minute until Gram said, "I smell the oatmeal burning."

They went into the kitchen, Gram bustling around to make tea, and Poppy leaning against the wall, his eyes closed. "I've thought about this," he said.

They sat there almost the whole morning talking, school forgotten. Poppy told them about his ship passing Rockaway, and seeing the Ferris wheel rising up in Playland like a ghost. He told them about France, and how he felt when he stood watching as the flame at the grave of the unknown soldier was lighted again.

Then at last, he reached into his pocket and pulled out

a small pile of pictures, Lily's mother in her wedding dress, Lily in the rowboat, Gram standing on the dock. Last was a picture of a girl in a Jeep. She was holding an umbrella and smiling.

"Ruth," Lily said, tracing the girl's face with her fingers.

"Ruth." Poppy leaned forward. "I took your letter . . ."

"Mine and Albert's," Lily said.

Poppy nodded. "I went to the convent, the Daughters of Wisdom, they're called . . ."

"And she was there."

"No." Poppy shook his head. "Albert's mother and father had written a newspaper in Hungary, a brave newspaper, and the nuns were afraid to keep her in Paris. Instead, they smuggled her out one night, and took her west, took her to a convent in Saint-Laurent, a convent with horses and cows and a river, the Sèvre . . ."

Poppy reached out for the picture, smiling. "She had a dozen mothers there. One to teach her English, one to teach her French, one to show her how to milk the cows and make cheese—"

"And did you see her?" Lily asked in a rush. "Did you tell her about Albert? Tell her about me?"

"Yes to all of that," he said. "I showed her your picture."

"And Albert . . ."

Poppy put his hand over hers. "She said she missed

Albert every day. She's waited through this whole war to go to Canada. She said she felt sad because she hadn't said goodbye to him."

Lily sat there looking at Poppy, wanting to ask what he had told Ruth, almost afraid to hear. "What . . . ?" she began.

"What did I say?" he asked her, smiling. "I told her that saying goodbye didn't matter, not a bit. What mattered were all the days you were together before that, all the things you remembered."

Lily took a deep breath. She squeezed Poppy's hand.

Chapter 27

1945

It was summer at last. Lily was wedged in the backseat of Poppy's old Ford with the suitcases, and bags, and rolled-up sweaters. Her feet, resting on Gram's tackle box, were tangled in a mess of fishing line.

They were going back to Rockaway, back to the house on stilts, back to the Atlantic Ocean at last.

The Ford had new tires now, and gas in the tank, and the three of them, Lily, Poppy, and Gram, sang all the way with the breeze coming in through the open windows. " 'Mairzy doats and dozy doats and liddle lamzy divy . . .' "

Lily knew they were almost there when they passed Margaret's house. The bottom-floor windows were still shuttered, but the one in the attic was shiny and almost black in the sun's reflection. Margaret wouldn't be there this summer, might never come back to Rockaway. Eddie was still lost somewhere in France, and Gram had heard that Mrs. Dillon couldn't bear to be there without him.

"Listen, Lily . . ." Gram turned in the front seat, tucking strands of her hair into her bun.

Lily could feel it even before she saw it: the bridge, and the galumping sound as the tires hit each plank.

"It's saying, 'Wel-come back, wel-come back.' " Gram raised her plump arms in the air. "Alleluia."

Lily nodded a little, but the bridge wasn't saying that for her. It was saying, "Al-bert's gone, Al-bert's gone."

She pressed her forehead against the car window, staring at the marshes, watching a seagull as it swooped down toward the pale reeds. She didn't want Gram or Poppy to know her eyes were prickling and her throat was tight.

"The same," Poppy said. "I told you. It's all the same."

Lily and Gram looked at each other, nodding, remembering. It would never be the same.

And then they were there. She hardly waited for the car to stop moving before she was out the back door, running for the sand and the water. She kicked off her shoes and left them on the empty boardwalk, peeling off her socks halfway across the beach.

Today the water was almost calm. Tiny waves folded over on themselves, then slid out to sea, leaving small fingers of foam on the damp sand.

Lily waded in, bunching up her skirt. The water was icy cold on her feet and ankles, numbing. She looked out at the gray triangular rock that jutted out near the end of the jetty, the place where she and Albert had first looked for Europe.

Suppose she never saw Albert again?

She leaned over to cup her hands in the water, to splash a little on her face. Her skirt, let loose, plastered itself against her legs.

She dug her toes into the sandy bottom, picturing her words sliding out to sea the way the waves did out to Europe. "You're my best friend, Albert," she whispered, "the best friend I ever had . . ."

Then Poppy was in back of her, his strong hands around her shoulders, pulling her into the dry warmth of his shirt.

They stood there for another moment before they went back toward the boardwalk together, Lily picking up one sock, looking around for the other one.

And then she saw the cat, standing there, watching her, ready to run.

Lily could feel the dryness in her mouth, the sand beginning to blow against her face, stinging. "Paprika?" she asked. Slowly she held out her hand.

Chapter 28

"Poppy, look," Lily said. "It's Albert's cat. The Orbans must have kept her after Albert went back to Canada."

Lily climbed the boardwalk steps slowly as the cat stood there, moving back a step each time she moved forward.

"It's me," Lily said, her hand out, reaching. "Don't you remember?"

And then the cat was in her arms, its orange coat short, and rough, and warm from the sun. Lily bent her head, rubbing her chin against the cat's head, listening to the sound of its rusty purring. She thought of Albert, and last summer, and Ruth.

Now the church bells were chiming five. Lily followed Poppy along the path to the house. Gram had opened the door and the windows on the porch. "Blowing the winter out," she said, looking up. "And here's Albert's cat."

Still holding the cat, Lily wandered out to the porch and leaned on the screen. She smelled the bay and listened to the water lapping against the pilings.

Someone was fishing from a rowboat, probably one of the kids from Broad Channel. Lily raised her arm to wave, and smiled as the girl waved back.

Under her feet, the porch floor was gritty. Any minute Gram would be calling, telling her to give it a quick sweep, and find the sheets, and get her bed ready. Lily reached for her book and flipped through until she found the star. She had taken it off her ceiling last night as she packed. She put a dab of glue on it and pasted it behind the bed with the others, smiling a little. Then she went into the kitchen for the broom.

"It's Friday night," Gram said over her shoulder. "The Orbans want us to come for dinner. Wash your face and . . ."

Lily didn't wait to hear the rest. Mrs. Orban would know about Albert and Ruth. She went into the bathroom quickly to comb her hair and run water over her hands. The water came in spurts at first, the way it always did after the winter. Lily leaned forward to look in the mirror, wondering if she looked different this year. She closed her eyes, remembering that Friday night last summer, getting ready to go to the Orbans', and Gram holding the washcloth over her red eyes, after she'd cried for Poppy. And she thought about Albert, with his dark hair and blue eyes.

If only Albert were there.

Lily thought about her problem list for the first time in a long time. *Lies*, and *Daydreaming*, and *Friends*, *need*. She didn't lie anymore. Every time she started to lie, she thought of Albert and closed her mouth. She still daydreamed, though. Sister Benedicta had told her that all writers did that, and that as long as you knew the difference between lies and daydreams you were in good shape.

Now Gram was knocking at the bathroom door. "Poppy's gone down to the Orbans' ahead of us," she said, "and if you don't hurry in there, the dinner will be ruined. They're all waiting . . ."

Lily made a face in the mirror, then scooped up a handful of water for her face. "I'm ready," she said, "ready now."

They walked down to the Orbans' on the road side, the tufts of grass bright against the sand, Lily carrying the cat along with her.

Halfway down the road, Lily could smell the fish cooking. She could hear Poppy talking, and the rumble of Mr.

Orban's voice. Mr. Orban's Ford was in the driveway, the headlights still painted black. She'd help him scrape them off first thing tomorrow.

Gram was looking toward her, and leaned over suddenly to kiss Lily's cheek. "It was a long war, a terrible war," she said, "but sometimes, even in the worst times, something lovely happens."

"What . . . ," Lily began. She reached up to feel her cheek, the first time she could ever remember Gram kissing her when it wasn't time to leave for school, or to go to bed.

She put her arms around Gram. *"Szeretlek,"* she whispered so softly she didn't know if Gram had heard.

And then she saw that Gram was pointing, nodding at her, and smiling. Lily looked toward the Orbans' house, almost knowing what she was going to see, not believing it could really happen, that it wasn't just Mrs. Orban waiting at the door. She thought about the cat. Of course Albert had kept the cat. That meant . . .

And there he was with the same mop of dark hair, and those bright blue eyes, and next to him, a girl with the same eyes, and she was smiling too.

Lily stopped to kiss Gram, and then she was walking toward them, feeling a little shy, but only for a moment, because Albert was pulling Ruth down the steps, and she could hear him saying, "It's Lily, it's my best friend, Lily."

Dear Reader:

I truly hope you've enjoyed reading Lily's story.

It seems that Lily's world has always been in my head. I've wanted to write about that world for years. Rockaway Beach, the Atlantic Ocean, ships steaming in convoys toward Europe, and the Second World War were part of my childhood. I remember the summer of 1944, remember the invasion and the news of the allied armies as they marched across France and liberated Paris late that August. I remember the fears of that time, and how personal it all was. I was surprised that other people, sometimes even adults, thought about the same things I did and had much the same worries. But most of all, I remember that friendship, in the secret world of childhood, added comfort and joy and was the very texture of my life.

I've written about friendship before, but in a lighthearted way, laughing as I've worked through the lives of Casey, Tracy & Company and the Polk Street Kids. But this time, I wanted to explore what happens to people as they forge a relationship in a more serious way. I wanted to tell my readers that even though the times are different now, people have always worried about the same things . . . loss and separation, the future, and sometimes war. I want readers to know that love and friendship make a difference.

Patricia Reilly Giff

Be sure to read Patricia Reilly Giff's latest novel

Excerpt from *Nory Ryan's Song* by Patricia Reilly Giff

Copyright © 2000 by Patricia Reilly Giff

Published by Delacorte Press

an imprint of

Random House Children's Books

a division of Random House, Inc.

1540 Broadway, New York, New York 10036

CHAPTER
1

Someone was calling.

"Nor-ry. Nor-ry Ry-an."

I was halfway along the cliff road. With the mist coming up from the sea, everything on the path below had disappeared.

"Wait, Nory."

I stopped. "Sean Red Mallon?" I called back, hearing his footsteps now.

"I have something for us," he said as he reached me. He pulled a crumpled bit of purple seaweed out of his pocket to dangle in front of my nose.

"Dulse." I took a breath. The smell of the sea was in it, salty and sweet. I was so hungry I could almost feel the taste of it on my tongue.

"Shall we eat it here?" he asked, grinning, his red hair a mop on his forehead.

"It'll be over and gone in no time," I said, and pointed up. "We'll go to Patrick's Well."

We reached the top of the cliffs with the rain on our heads. *"I am Queen Maeve,"* I sang, twirling away from the edge. *"Queen of old Ireland."*

I loved the sound of my voice in the fog, but then I loved anything that had to do with music: the Ballilee church bells tolling, the rain pattering on the stones, even the *carra-crack* of the gannets calling as they flew overhead.

I scrambled up to Mary's Rock. As the wind tore the mist into shreds, I could see the sea, gray as a selkie's coat, stretching itself from Ireland to Brooklyn, New York, America.

Sean came up in back of me. "We will be there one day in Brooklyn."

I nodded, but I couldn't imagine it. Free in Brooklyn. Sean's sister, Mary Mallon, was there right now. Someone had written a letter for her, and Father Harte had read it to us. Horses clopped down the road, she said, bringing milk in huge cans. And no one was ever hungry. Even the sound of it was wonderful. Brook-lyn.

The rain ran along the ends of my hair and into my neck. I shook my head to make the drops fly and thought of my da on a ship, the rain running down his long dark hair too. Da, who was far away, fishing to pay the rent. He had been gone for weeks, and it would be months before he came home again.

I swallowed, wishing for Da so hard I had to turn my head to hide my face from Sean. I blew a secret kiss across the waves; then we picked our way up the steep little path to Patrick's Well.

We sat ourselves down on one of the flat stones around the well and leaned over to look into the water. People with money threw in coins for prayers. But the well was endlessly deep, wending its way down through the cliffs toward the sea, and it took ages for coins to sink to the bottom. Granda said that might be why it took so long for those prayers to be answered.

But not many people had coins to drop into the well. Instead there was the tree overhead. People tied their prayers to the branches: a piece of tattered skirt, the edge of a collar.

"I see my mother's apron string." Sean pointed up as he tore a bit of dulse in two and handed me half.

I nodded, sucking on a curly edge. I looked up at the tree. A strip of my middle sister Celia's shift was hanging there. Now, what did that one want? She had no shame. There it was, a piece of her underwear left to wag in the wind until it rotted away. Every creature who walked by would be gaping at it.

I stood up quickly, moving around to the other side of the well to look down at our glen. The potato fields were covered with purple blossoms now, and stone walls zig-zagged up and down between.

And then, something else.

"Sean," I said, "what's happening down there?"

Absently he tore the last bit of dulse in two. "Men," he said slowly. "Bailiffs with a battering ram. Someone is being put out of a house."

Someone. I knew who it was. A quick flash of the little beggar, Cat Neely, her curly hair covering most of her face. And Cat's mother, who sat in their yard, teeth gone, cheeks sunken, with no money to pay the rent.

"Don't think about it," Sean said, his hand on my shoulder, his face sad. "There's nothing can be done."

"Coins," I said. "If only someone . . ." I broke off. I knew it myself. No one in the glen had an extra penny. Not Sean's family. Not mine. My older sister Maggie and Sean's brother Francey were saving every bit they could to get married. But even that would take years.

The dulse on my tongue tasted bitter now. Cunningham, the English lord, owned all our land, all our houses; he could put any of us out if he wanted. And now it would be Cat and her mother.

There was someone with a coin, I knew that.

Anna Donnelly.

Sean and I were afraid of her. He had said that one of the *sidhe* might live under her table. I shuddered, thinking of those beings from the other world. *Tangles of gray hair, bony fingers pointing, crouched in the darkness.* Anna had magic in her, too. She could heal up a wen on the finger, or straighten a bone with her weeds, but only when she wanted to.

And she hadn't saved my mam the day my little brother, Patch, was born.

That Anna Donnelly had a coin.

And I was the only one who knew about it.

I thought of the day I had stopped near her house. The thatch on her roof was old and plants grew green over the top. And there was Anna outside, teetering on a stool, her white hair in wisps around the edge of her cap. She had peered over her shoulder, her face as wrinkled as last year's potatoes, then held something up before she shoved it deep into the thatch.

I had seen the glint of it, the shine.

The coin.

And in my mind now: I could save Cat Neely and her mother. If only Anna would give me that coin.

Suddenly my mouth was dry.

I turned to Sean. "Thank you for the dulse," I said, and left him there, mouth open, as I flew down the path away from the cliff.

CHAPTER
2

I hurled myself along the road, thinking about the bailiffs and Devlin, who collected the rents for Lord Cunningham. They'd tear down the roof of the Neely house and pound at the beam until it splintered in over the hearth. Nothing would be left but dust, and chunks of limestone, and bits of thatch settling on the floor.

Cat would be sobbing, her tiny face blotched, and her mother rocking back and forth outside, both of them with nowhere to go. Devlin would never let them stay with another family. "Lord Cunningham wants to clear this land," he'd say, "not add more faces to each house."

I crossed our own field, seeing my sister Maggie drawing a picture on the wall of the house. Three-year-old

Patch was dancing around her. "Me," he was saying. "It's my face."

They didn't see me, and I didn't stop. What would I say to Anna? I wondered. *My da will be home soon, long before the rent is due,* I'd tell her. *We will give you back the coin straightaway. But right now we could save Cat and her mother.* Even the thought of knocking on her door dried my mouth and dampened my hands. But if she said yes I could bring the coin to Cat and put it into her little fist. When she opened her hand, her mother would see it.

I picked up my skirt and catercornered across Anna's field, one hand covering the stitch in my side. I could feel my fingers trembling. I went up the path then, before I could change my mind, rapped hard on the door, and stepped back.

Nothing happened. I leaned forward and knocked again. The door stayed shut. Where was Anna? Where had she gone? Was someone's baby being born in one of the far glens?

From far away I heard the men shouting. I went out to the path to see if she was coming. *Please come, Anna Donnelly. Please.*

I turned and looked back at the thatch. The coin was right there. It was so close I could climb up and reach for it.

And then the door opened.

My hand flew to my mouth. I stepped back, so frightened I hardly remembered why I was there.

Anna stared at me with faded blue eyes, her head to one side.

I opened my mouth, but I couldn't speak.

She took a step outside, listening to the men shouting in the distance. "They are putting the Neelys on the road?" Her lips were puckered, with deep lines around her mouth.

"Lend me a coin for them," I said in a rush. "I will pay you."

"And how will you do that?"

"My da will be back. He'll give it to you. I know he will."

A louder sound in the distance. Was the house going under?

Anna looked up, thinking, frowning. "I will give you the coin," she said, "but you will pay for it another way."

Don't miss the year's most hilarious and unforgettable journey . . .

The Watsons Go to Birmingham—1963

Christopher Paul Curtis

1996 Newbery Honor Book

YEARLING NEWBERY

ISBN: 0-440-41412-1

Follow the adventures of the Weird Watsons—Momma, Dad, little sister Joetta, Kenny, and Byron—as they set out on a trip like no other. They're heading south to Birmingham, Alabama—toward one of the darkest moments of American history. . . .

Now in Paperback from Yearling Books!

Molly Fletcher
=
Star Searcher